Extinct at Last

The memoirs of Robert Clarke Esq. (Clubman)

Christopher Dalton

iUniverse, Inc.
New York   Bloomington

Extinct at Last
The memoirs of Robert Clarke Esq. (Clubman)

iUniverse books may be ordered through booksellers or by contacting:

iUniverse
1663 Liberty Drive
Bloomington, IN 47403
www.iuniverse.com
1-800-Authors (1-800-288-4677)

*Because of the dynamic nature of the Internet, any Web addresses or
links contained in this book may have changed since publication and may
no longer be valid. The views expressed in this work are solely those of
the author and do not necessarily reflect the views of the publisher, and
the publisher hereby disclaims any responsibility for them.*

ISBN: 978-1-4401-4291-8 (pbk)
ISBN: 978-1-4401-4292-5 (ebk)

Library of Congress Control Number: 2009937476

Printed in the United States of America

iUniverse rev. date: 12/11/2009

Written in the Upstairs Bar at the Badminton and Racquet Club

over the course of several years. My thanks to the faithful bar

staff who attended to my every need.

Signed;   Robert Clarke Esq. (Clubman)

This is the diary of Mr. Robert Clarke. I cannot defend his treatment of women, but the document does, however, have anthropological and historical value and must be thought of as a time capsule.

It was Robert's express wish that his jottings not be made public for a hundred years. However, following a fatal car accident outside his club, Mr. Clarke's diary was found amongst his belongings within his club locker.

Because of a lawsuit brought by some of his relatives over his final will, the estate has been forced to raise money. Therefore the recipients of his will, a grateful Club staff, have decided to publish this document.

Yours truly;

Gerald Lewis, Solicitor, Family Law Practice. (Lewis & Grade)

CHAPTER 1

(1966 and all that is the place Robert Clarke starts his diary. I have endeavoured to remove the more litigious material, and the contents jump from era to era, but I have tried not to interfere with his writing "style." Ed)

Why shouldn't I be happy? Mrs. A is snuggling against my leg and her daughter Grace is kissing me and all of us are naked. God, how I loved 1966. Of course this particular tableau ended in tears, as these things do, but it was marvelous, if a little strained. I was thinking of Mrs. A the other day, and I have to say she was ahead of her time. A woman of her colouring walked near me downtown and it instantly put me in mind of her. A woman of a certain age perfumed by her experience is a Scud missile to me.

Let me first clear up the mother-daughter thing. Like all fantasies, this was better imagined than actual. It reminds me of the time I appeared late at an orgy (my one and only) in the Hollywood Hills on Doheny Drive. All I could think of was "Who has the dirty feet?"

More later, but first I have begun to think that it is high time for someone of my ilk to tell the true story of our time, of those of us that were born just after the war. Who were we? What were we like? What happened to that era? So I, Robert Clarke, have taken up my usual spot at the indoor balcony of my club, where I have a bird's eye-view, more like a vulture's,

1

many of the late morning women making their way to the badminton courts would say. It soothes the soul watching the next generation of beauties pass by, although they will never know the charms I was once blessed with.

We are all well into our sixties and yet still called the "Boomers." This, of course, is nonsense. To say we are the same as the wretched children born in 1960 beggars the imagination. No, we were born in 1945 and 1946, and our war-sickened fathers and mothers were trying to get to know each other after years of separation. I am not the same as someone born in the 1960s; they did not flog children by then, more is the pity.

I first saw light because my dear mother got my father pie-eyed and herself pregnant before that poor besotted man could get up the nerve to say, "What ho, old thing, I have been having an affair with Lady Bennett, whose late husband was pranged up a bit in the Battle of Britain, so I'm off back to Blighty. Awfully decent of you to be so understanding, what?"

Mother was not stupid. She had heard the stories from the other wives about her husband's comfortable hospital stay with the newly widowed nurse in London after D-Day, so she was ready when he hesitantly got off the troop train at Union Station. A large suite had been booked at the Royal York with champagne galore. I am sure that father, like me, would have thought, "Oh, what the hell, might as well give her one before I tell the poor thing."

After that Father had a triumphant return to the neighbourhood as a war hero, which he certainly was, and into his favourite chair at his cozy home and hearth. However I am sure there was a great deal of "Darling, we simply must talk. I have something awfully important to say, old thing." Father had affected an upper-class accent to suit his English rose. Mother, no doubt through gritted teeth, would answer, "Not now, darling, we are due at the Taylors", putting off the pleas from Father until the day she swanned into his study and announced that she was heavy with child so he could tell his English popsy to find some other idiot! Father quickly sent off the cowardly telegram: "OOPS, CAN'T COME. STOP. CLARKE."

No doubt thousands of returning soldiers were doing exactly the same thing. However, like my father, many of those same soldiers had been absorbed by the Brits and all things British and so desired that their wanted or in this case unwanted children brought up as if we lived in Essex or Kent. (I apologize in advance for my inability to stay the course as far as a train of thought is concerned. I have always moved around too much, but in the end I have to amuse myself or nothing much seems to come out, plus my mind wanders naturally. I have my Birks pen and leather notepad at the ready and I am poised to begin. Back to 1966.)

Grace A. attended Branksome Hall girls' school in Toronto's Rosedale neighbourhood. Her family lived a little north, above the tracks in the cheaper part of Rosedale, Moore Park. I met Grace at the May Fair, held each year at Rosedale Park, famous for being the home of the first Grey Cup. I had seen her before in the shapeless middy those dreadful schools forced upon unsuspecting girls, much to the relief of fretting fathers. Girls' bodies are remarkable. When they are 12, they are awkward things, sexless and bookish. One would have a hard time imagining a future where a besotted lover, mad for their favours. would promise them anything, and if he were me, he would be lying but very earnest. However it is quite a different story by the time they reach 16.

I saw Grace by the used book display in the outdoor hockey rink. The display was looked after by two frightful women, Mrs. McGibben and her sister Miss McCutchen, both with moustaches that reminded me of retired hussars. They worked at the Deer Park Library where as jammy-faced children we would sit in a circle while they would read stories through fetid breath. Awful. Still I enjoyed Treasure Island, The Scarlet Pimpernel and such, especially watching the two sisters act out the parts in strange accents.

"Hello, Master Clarke," they twittered. Grace didn't notice. She was holding a book about the Shetland Islands. I moved over to her right, waited till she purchased the book and then put on my look. My "look" was just this side of Lord Byron with dyspepsia, writer's block and losing his mother's pet cat. It would have to be a very unfeeling girl to have waved me away. It helped that I was fairly attractive, slim, in my early 20s, and she at 16 was perhaps already stirring sexually.

I have found during this long trip called life that referring to the Romantic poets brings a girl's emotions to a head. Once you establish that you also have urgent feelings for the same stanzas so beloved by said girl, you can move on to such things as pacifism and vegetarianism. Once we have stormed that beach, it is only a hop, skip and jump to being free and without clothes.

Perhaps I had not mentioned that Grace dressed in mufti was a staggering sight. When you looked at her figure, you knew there was a God, for this was not a random bit of Darwinism. This had been worked on long and hard, with great blueprints. So there I stood, between her and the exit, until she bumped into me. "Sorry," she said.

I continued to stare off into the mid-horizon, as if I heard a distant bagpipe softly lamenting near a loch.

"I am sorry also," I replied finally. "I was not paying attention, for I was thinking those short trees over there remind me so much of the Scottish Islands I visited during the Easter holidays." I then stared at my feet so that I looked abashed, very much like an artist who can't afford paint. Grace gave a quiver or two.

"Did you say the Scottish Isles?"

"Yes — why?"

I had learned from my older sister never to stare at breasts if you are planning on closing any deals. She claimed it put girls off. I kept my eyes away from her pillow-like chest.

It seemed appropriate to stroll towards the gate and away from those harpies and their books. As we walked, Grace began to question me about the islands, about which I didn't have a clue, except there were little horses bounding about the place.

How badly did I wish to see her cotton shorts or bra, as this might be the best I could do under the present circumstances? Very badly, I decided.

I would have to visit the aforementioned harpies and swipe a book on the place. In the meantime I sort of fluttered around the point that I didn't know anything at all and looked a bit hurt at her insistence at knowing where I had stayed and who I met. I managed to totter towards the nearby ravine as if seeking respite from the crowd at the fair. I knew the ravine well. When I was a child, this was where our forts were, the theatre of cowboy and Indian fights.

It was also a place where Ivan Deschamp, my dearest friend at 12, and I staged a huge battle between Rob Roy and the English for our cub troop, 89B. The Akela was a Scot, Jock Stuart, who was mad as a fruit fly, but Ivan and I needed a few more badges to qualify for cub camp that summer. We had failed sewing and semaphore (how did we know some old lady who had been in the navy would know that Ivan and I had spelled FUCK YOU BADEN-POWELL with our little flags on parent night?).

Ivan had come up with the plan and put it to Mr. Stuart, who virtually spat out his joy that in the heartland of conservative Toronto, the truth would out about the hated English. Ivan's thought was to round up the younger brothers and sisters from the neighbourhood and dragoon them into playing the English and the Scots, with us as the respective leaders. Every household had kilts from girls' schools; even the red blazers for our English invaders were from the girls (St.

Clements). So we dressed everyone in appropriate gear and explained the plan. The English would march along the ravine road and at a signal, the kids dressed as Scottish Highlanders would rush down a steep slope and slaughter the Redcoats. We had no idea whether this had actually happened, but the man who gave us our badges seemed to think it did. Ivan, quite wrongly as it turned out, refused a full-scale rehearsal. We made do with the Redcoats marching on the road while the Scottish got to stand on the hill and shout abuse at those below. We had by then decided we would both be on the British side as it entailed less running. The tension amongst the Rosedale offspring was mounting and there were a few fights, but we managed to keep the lid on till the selected Saturday.

What became known as the Rosedale Riot started pleasantly enough on a blistering hot day. Word had gotten out amongst the parents, who streamed in from the surrounding streets with blankets to watch from the north hill of the ravine. There must have been more than a hundred children, with quite a few parents sprawled upon the green slopes. At Mr. Stuart's signal, everybody took their positions. Ivan showed a little uneasiness at some of the aggression being demonstrated by the older Scottish boys toward the younger British kids below them. We had thought there would be fewer accidents if the older boys were the ones to run down the hill with the younger ones safely on the road, fewer falls, etc. Mr. Stuart was raring to go as the British started to march with their hockey sticks, painted black, as muskets.

Ivan gave a gasp and pointed. I looked and my heart sank. The Scottish ranks now filled the top of the north hill and they were armed, many with family regalia, some with huge broadswords and a whole school of thought with pikes. Several parents got to their feet in alarm as the howls of the Scottish kids filled the valley. The English on the road knew something was up when they saw Ivan and me headed past them and up the opposite slope. Just then Mr. Stuart dropped the flag and with a roar the kids on the hill started to run towards the road. As the English side started to retreat, the hill hooligans as a herd adjusted their path to the right, directly into scores of now truly alarmed parents. One of them, clearly a business executive of some sort stood up and said to the advancing hordes, "Now see here, if we …."

He got no further outside a bellowed "woof" before he was carried down the hill. It was the Scots advancing with a wall of parental seersucker in front that really frightened the Brits below. Kids could be seen tearing off their red coats with their fathers' and grandfathers' medals still attached and making a dash for it. The parents had formed into sort of a ball that was gaining speed with a mind to having a short, frank chat with Mr. Stuart, who was laying into the English kids with his flag.

Ivan and I had gained the high ground on the other side and from our perch could safely watch the battle below. It became difficult to make out what was happening as the dust from the battle rose in the once quiet valley. However, we could see enough to loosen a bowel or two. Parents, realizing there would be no assistance from anyone else, began to circle the wagons. Tiny groups of them formed in the midst of the chaos, mothers alone in several and fathers in others. Cries of "Wait till I get you home" and "What the devil is the meaning of this?" rang out. In one scene of unintended democracy a butler and his master were swept away as one, holding hands.

By this point, Mr. Stuart had begun to have second thoughts. His real job was working for the city, in the hydro as something or other, and while his pay was not large, it came with the promise of a pension, which would go a long way to providing a comfortable life in his beloved Highlands. Looking around, he seemed to see that his longed-for pension had grown wings; also the dreaded Mrs. Stuart came to mind, which galvanized him into action. But it was like stopping the Queen Mary at full steam — it would take time.

Gradually, with the help of outraged parents and the odd policeman, the combatants were separated and the damage assessment begun. The English boys were huddled amongst the scrubby bushes on the near slope, of which one had to say was not a pleasant sight, many cuts and bruises, etc. On the far slope, the Scottish kids, while still braying at the Brits, had at least started to listen to reason and began to suck on the Mackintosh toffee supplied earlier by the company's owner.

Ivan and I, being the cowards that we were, claimed we had been knocked senseless in the melee and were exonerated. Our grateful parents took us home, no more was said about it and I returned to my school, Ridley. Not so for poor Mr. Stuart. There was talk of a horsewhipping, we never saw him again and the cubs had a new leader the following week. Just for a moment I would like to speak to him again, but of course he is long dead. as I am now in my 60s.

Oh, I know, Grace, what the hell happened to Grace? A master (teacher) at school used to say my concentration could be depended on to wander during a lesson. Grace took my hand and we entered the ravine. She babbled on about crofters and such as we went down the slope to a shady overhang near the battle scene I mentioned. I suggested we sit there because it put me in mind of a place like it in the highlands near Edinburgh. I hadn't a clue but nor did she. When she finally took a breath… I kissed her. That startled her, I can tell you, but I told her I was so overcome with the romance of it all and that her eyes had pulled me toward her (my sister had told me to mention the eyes because apparently girls enjoyed that more that being told it was their giant breasts and you had a boner) so I had no choice, and she said it was all right to kiss her again. What do girls think? That we want to really go for a walk? Don't they know we are going to give it a try? We are not listening!

That glorious Saturday was all around the mulberry bush but no skin actually touched. It turned out a wise move not to push it too far and be content with massaging her gorgeous chest. The first girls that I really got to touch, not just glancing blows mind, were Catholic girls and they certainly seemed to enjoy themselves. It must have been all the repressed guilt or something. Anglican girls had little pointy breasts that they shielded like the Crown Jewels and if you ever managed to get near them, as I once did with Diana Bute before going back to boarding school (I told her she had to give back my school ring if I didn't get a feel) were found to be hard and uninviting or with Kleenex stuffed in their bras. The one voluptuous exception was Deb Sharp from Bishop Strachan School, the girls' school next to our rivals, Upper Canada College.

She always went out with UCC boys and as my school was in St. Catharines, I rarely got to see her, but there was a certain promise in her eyes whenever I ran into her. The day finally came that we agreed to go to a movie. In those days one could sit in the smoking loges up top at the back and be very private, particularly at the old Glendale Theatre on Avenue Road. The movie started and I put my arm around her. Now, as every boy knows, you must rest your arm on the back of the seat so as not to put too much weight on the girl's neck. However after a few minutes, tingles start to run up and down your arm because the back of the seat fits nicely into your funny bone at the elbow. This is an age-old problem, but males have learned to deal with it by moving the fingers continually. Unfortunately, I was rather enjoying the movie and not moving the old digits much. It was a Burt Lancaster western in which the leading actress had the sharpest bra in Christendom. I was fascinated by its shape and aerodynamics. We were sailing along with Burt having dispatched two or three bad guys and the rest saddling up to come to town and sort him out — it had something to do with cattle-ranching vs. sheep ranching, and all the gentlefolk were sheep ranchers with big-breasted daughters and they were the ones who needed Burt's help. Just then dear Deb leaned towards me, whispering, "You can if you want."

There was no time to waste, for Burt was strapping on his gun belt for the climax, meaning I had to work fast before the lights came up. I moved my hand down to cover her right one and …at least that was the signal I had sent to my white and bloodless limb, which was still sitting there on its perch looking back at me. I sent another one: "Captain to mate, move NOW!" Nothing. I had no feeling in my hand and what was worse, none in my arm. It was as if I were speaking to someone-else's sleeve. My expectant date looked at me and I looked past her at my dead arm. In a panic I used my other arm to lift up the recalcitrant one and bang it on the seat back.

Apparently film devotees do not, as the climax approaches, like to be distracted by a fool banging his arm as if he were Dr. Strangelove. Debby began to look alarmed, as did the man on the other side of her as my dead appendage kept hitting him. Result, no satisfaction, plus a strange reputation descended upon me.

CHAPTER 2

(Robert's greatest regret, Ruth, and his deep love of cricket....and a bit about his old Pater. Ed.)

Just so that you don't think little Robert was in sexual anguish at all times, there was girl called Ruth Hallry who used to hang around the Toronto Cricket, Curling and Skating Club, watching us practice cricket over the summer holidays under the watchful eye of Mohamed Khan, the former opening bowler for Pakistan. Ruth took figure skating lessons at the club from a top pro and was expected to place well in the world tournament two years hence. Her lessons started at 6:30 a.m. six days a week with no exceptions, all year. We private school boys, on the other hand, would arrive the worse for wear around 10:30 a.m. Mr. Khan was beside himself and would wave his sweater above his head in frustration. He could not get past the idea that we would drink in one evening the GNP of the average family in his poor benighted country.

Cricket was not a popular game in Canada even then, but we got free membership at the club if we showed up, and as it was well known to have the comeliest of women, we showed up. The problem for cricket in Canada, then as now, is youth, for it is a "greying" game. In a panic the club would fish at all the private schools, looking for student cricket players to augment the dwindling older ones through the summer. They would bring a pro over from some Third World cricket power, and would insist that we attend 10 o'clock nets during the week. When Ruth got a break from her training, she would wander out into the sunshine to watch us. She was greeted with low wolf whistles from the slobbering teenage boys under the tutelage of the sweater-waving East Asian(he seemed to wave it whenever we became to much for him, perhaps it was a big deal where he came from but we just laughed)

I look back on this as one of the most wonderful summers one could imagine. We lived the life of Riley, with money from parents, cars from parents, free housing from parents …we were 16, blond and tanned, and happy. The one thing I would change is the way we treated poor Mr. Khan. He believed that men were put on this earth for one thing and one thing only: cricket. He had played since he was two and saw no reason why every other man should not take it as seriously as he did. We did not. We loved the game but also realized it was Canada, and baseball ruled. But still we were glamorous. Dressed all in creamy white, bronzed and young — most girls had only seen cricketers as fat old men in dirty white ducks, not this. We certainly struck Ruthy as different and fascinating, Gods from the other side of the tracks if you will. Every day she took her place on a bench just to the right of the nets, watching us with her big blue eyes, or should I say Higgens and me. Higgens was a wonderful specimen of his class (mid-upper) with tousled blond hair, piercing grey eyes, a blistering smile and full lips. Add to that his six-foot frame and you had widespread jealousy amongst the rest of us. I was simply pleasant to look at, with more of a puppy-dog friendliness. There was something cruel about Higgens, perhaps around his eyes. One didn't see it at first but it was there, as his terribly bloody but successful business career has borne out.

Many people from the club would traipse by the nets on their way to the tennis courts, including the infamous Mrs. A. Oh, dear, I left her and Grace a few pages back, didn't I? A master at Ridley always complained about my concentration, or lack thereof. This was indeed the first time I became aware of Mrs. A and her daughter, but I'll get back to them. Anyway, after a week or so of Ruthy showing some interest in the two of us, Higgens left for his cottage in Georgian Bay and I had the field to myself. Ruthy was not a beauty in the Hollywood meaning of the word but she was pretty. A healthy rich complexion, plus a skater's body with long muscular legs, a fairly large behind with perky breasts and best of all, she was keen on yours truly. There was one awful exception: her teeth. Back then not everyone went to an orthodontist, even if they knew what they were. The attitude in many of the not-so-well-off families was "So what?" Like us, Ruthy got a free pass for the club, but our families could have afforded to join if they had wanted to, unlike hers. This was my first experience with someone who was poor (the club provided her lessons for free as a scholarship). I did not care about any of that in the initial weeks. Ruthy let me kiss her the first time we went for a walk at the lunch break, over by the groundskeeper's shed near the pool. Two days later, I was exploring her chest while she was stroking my erection through my cotton cricket trousers behind the squash courts. Holy noodle, I loved Ruthy.

By the Thursday of the second week of this, our passion was threatening to get us kicked out of the Cricket, Skating and Curling Club. I don't know if any of you have ever had to bowl the opening over against a schoolboy team from Ireland with an erection? It's bloody uncomfortable, I can tell you. The guys started calling me Tripod and the general populace began to cast an alarmed eye towards the two of us. Several older clubmen approached me, advising "Steady on, old boy."

My only point in bringing up Ruthy was that she was the first girl who allowed me to truly explore a female body in my own time. Her mother worked in nursing and she and Ruthy shared a small two-bedroom near Avenue Road and Wilson. I don't remember whether she even had a father; I must not have cared.

We spent delightful hours together looking at and touching each other, although she wouldn't go all the way. Her mother was very keen on sharing information about how disgusting and filthy men were in general. To some degree I shared her concerns if by filthy she meant unsanitary, as I had lived then almost exclusively at boys' schools most of my life, and I can tell you of sights I witnessed that would have given pause to a Mongol. I, of course, was immaculately clean, following my sister's instructions. Anyway, I would like to thank you, Ruthy, for being the first girl in my life to stop squirming long enough for me to have a really good look. Of course it did not end well. It became obvious to even the meanest of intellects that I just wanted to go to her apartment and nowhere else. I did not want to be seen publicly with her or, I am sorry to say, her friends. So for weeks I would come up with outlandish excuses not to take her to movies or dinners. Finally even a gentle fawn such as Ruthy had had enough. I was beginning to realize that I was entering my wicked period and to this day there are those who say they look forward to my emergence from that period. Very funny. What 16-year- old boy isn't wicked when there is much to be wicked about? I know today you simply get your trousers down without taking your hat off, but then, in the Dark Ages, one had to be cunning and since I was a bit thick, I had to be wicked instead, in order to seduce.

Our last name was Clarke, with the E, if you please, as my dear mother was apt to say, and Father's company made furniture in several plants across Canada. It was a bit down market really, especially after the war, but good enough to make it into Eaton's, which was all that really mattered to Father: to get it into Eaton's and Simpson's. To be fair, they couldn't get the work done inexpensively enough to beat out the Yank stuff that was coming in, and everyone wanted American in those days. The unions would also make my father sputter; according to him, they were all run by malingering Scots. Clarke Furniture had gone along its merry way for 120 years, producing inexpensive copies of a Sheridan or Morris-style dining room table or drawing room settee that suited the tastes of the grey Canadian market tastes. In New England, flinty-eyed Yankee merchants cast their gazes northward, straight into the Clarke Furniture market. Father was worried, as usual, about it one night when I asked for the company hockey tickets; he mumbled into his martini and handed them to me from the inside pocket of one of the Tip Top suits his brother made him buy every year. My uncle James was a vice-president at Tip Top Tailors, which sounds great, but Father would refer to, with dismay, as a job fit only for "Yids". Ye gods.

Father learned his lesson years later. He sat on the board of directors of Canadian Breweries, invited by E.P. Taylor as a reward for his sterling war service. Taylor had been one of those one-dollar-a- year men during the war, a gang of business barons working under the auspices of C.D. Howe, known as the Minister of Everything. Someone told Father that Taylor had invented the toaster, but this was never verified. Anyway Taylor had asked my father to check out the new mall, Yorkdale, as a possible post for the Brewer's Retail to open a shop. Father returned a week late for the meeting, bursting through the boardroom door and announced, "Every Sheeny in town has a store there, and we should, too." Instead of the anticipated look of thanks on E.P.'s face, his countenance had fallen like an elevator.

"Charles," E.P. said, "I would like you to meet Mr. Lipshitz, who I have asked to have lunch with us as a guest of the board. Mr. Lipshitz is the part owner of several stores at Yorkdale."

Father always told these stories on himself as a lesson in how the world had changed and how we must too. When he wasn't angry with us, he was a lot of fun and we adored him. The one blunder my sister and I witnessed was a classic. It was after the grandstand show at the Canadian National Exhibition sometime in the mid-1950s, you know, the kind with Bob Hope and a posse of dancers and then the fireworks ending with the Queen and the sign that reminded us to drive carefully. Father would become extremely frustrated trying to extricate his car from the lot with 5,000 others. He had a VIP pass for everything, including free parking, but all the attendants had gone by then and what had been an orderly entrance became chaos upon leaving. Father described it as if someone dropped a pack of cigarettes at a Hungarian refugee camp.

The trick was to get out of the main lanes of traffic, bully your way to the outside and then scamper for the exit. The theory was that we would arrive at the exit earlier than those who had lined up in the main aisle and then some kind soul would let us in and out we would go. Father was at his best leading us from the building; we had broken new records for the middle-class 400-yard dash, although I thought I saw him elbow a slower family out of the way. Once at the car, amid shouts of recrimination about the fornicating bylaw-crazy aldermen who forced citizens through this every year, we were off in the family Jag.

We were doing rather well at the start of it all. People ran for their lives as Father shouted, "I didn't fight a war to wait two hours here." We rounded the last curve with the exit in sight. But just then a huge, dirty and badly painted car shot ahead of us from the other aisle. This caused a near accident, with three other cars slowly and legally making their way out. All came to a halt. Father rolled down his window (he did not believe in the new American invention of power windows) and began to shout at the car that had nipped us at the post. "Where did you get your license, you idiot, in a cereal box?" And "How did you enjoy your three years in Grade 5, you cretin?"

This carried on for some time, with my mother and sister encased in embarrassment but I rather enjoyed it; this was real-life excitement to a six-year-old. The door to the old junker started to open as my father had moved on to "This is what comes of having sexual congress with relatives, close relatives."

Actually he never finished the second "relatives," because he saw what we had seen slightly earlier. Father had the bad habit of playing to his audience, gauging his performance rather than watching his target. What we had become aware of was the largest human being I had ever seen until that moment, emerging from the hobo car. Mother said, "Oh dear."

Father quickly rolled up his window and looked in the rear-view mirror, but there was no escape as the behemoth came toward our car. Father had faced all sorts of adversities in his 36 years, particularly D-Day, Holland and Germany during the war, but I dare say nothing quite like this, not helped by the six-year-old boy in the back seat encouraging him to smack the "dumb monster."

The Dumb Monster now stood beside Father's window, looking down from a great height. Father slowly rolled down his window. "Yes, may I help you?" he said, rather quietly, I thought.

"Was that you yelling at me?" came the low rumble.

As my father pondered this question, the monster's wife appeared at my mother's window. They stared at each other. Mrs. Monster was as small as her husband was large, which brought another hoot of giggles from yours truly, snugly sitting behind the action. Suddenly there was a hand around my throat, which ended my loud giggling in mid-warble. Father gave me what can only be described as a death look.

Then he turned back to the main event as my mother made cooing noises through the window. I noticed a great crowd had gathered, mainly citizens who appeared to have spent the same three years in Grade 5 as the giant. Father sadly opened the door and got out as the monster cracked his knuckles in anticipation.

"I blame whatever you heard on the blasted echoes one gets from the proximity of the stadium wall and from all these cars endeavoring to exit at once, eh?" my father said.

"Wot?" said the foundation block. There were clearly several words in my father's sentence that were new to him. Father struck a winning stance, put on a happy smile and said: "So let's all return to our vehicles as the hour is late and be on our way."

"Wot?" he said again, visibly agitated, perhaps because of the absence of his matriculation.

Father was now pulled into the crowd and for several minutes we lost sight of him. Mother said, "Oh dear" again, but kept a fixed but pleasant smile as if a tea she was attending had run out of cake. As for me, I had stopped laughing, particularly after several urchins had crawled onto the trunk of the car and were staring at me like cats viewing an injured bird. All of a sudden a man stuck his head into the car.

"Don't worry, Mrs. Clarke, we'll get the Colonel back," he said, and with several of his kind, he shot into the crowd and disappeared.

"Oh dear," Mother repeated, but with the conviction that the cake was now on the way, for she knew these men were in Father's old regiment and would not rest till they had rescued their former CO. Eventually Father was passed back to us through the crowd. His tie had been cut in half, part of his suit lapel was ripped and a shoe was missing. He maintained his composure long enough to thank his men for releasing him. On the way home he spoke darkly of society's underclass and having to face what he suspected to be sodomites, as Mother tried to shush him in front of me. Father never spoke loudly about other drivers again, but he would mutter bitterly that he not fought a war to put up with this.

I know, Ruthy. I have not forgotten Ruthy. I had told her I would take her to Maple Leaf Gardens to see the Leafs play the Rangers. Summer had ended, the hockey season had begun, and life in Canada is always better when hockey starts. I thought taking Ruthy to that particular game would be the perfect way to shut her friends up, proving I had deep feelings for her. Nobody she knew had gone to the Gardens so it would be a huge <u>event</u> in her life, meaning I could live off this one treat for the rest of the affaire.

Conn Smythe had built Maple Leaf Gardens at the beginning of the Depression in 1930. He owned a quarry north of Toronto in Caledon, which allowed him all the materials he needed but not the work needed to build it. He got around it by paying some of the labour costs in futures or stock in the Gardens and it opened in 1933 with the Leafs against the Chicago Black Hawks. The Leafs promptly lost, but a love story had started between Canada and the team. It was a beautiful building with a soaring ceiling holding the broadcast studio, called the Gondola, where Foster Hewitt held Canadians in his hands while he called the games for first radio and then TV.

I had picked the game against the Rangers for my date with Ruthy because no one gave them much of a chance that year, so I thought that none of the families who sat next to our four seats would be there. I didn't really want to show Ruthy off at a good game like one against the Canadiens. With those teeth and what she could be depended on to wear, would make things awkward for me. Before I go any further, let the record show that I had the best of intentions. I don't think that will help me much when I'm standing there on Judgment Day, but it does me good to practice my defense. The good news is I don't believe in the Hereafter anyway.

Things that night went badly from the start. I pulled Dad's Jag up to Ruthy's apartment and strode in looking fairly sharp with my cricket blazer, club tie (Royal Canadian Yacht Club), grey flannels and penny loafers, looking forward to a time of passion with Ruthy if I could only live through the game. Her mother opened the door almost at my knock. I bowed and scraped, as I did with all my dates' parents, yet she seemed somewhat unhinged.

"Where is Ruthy, Mrs. Hallry?" I said jauntily.

"There has been a wee bit of a problem," she replied. She licked her lips several times. "You see," she began, but then followed my bug-eyed stare. Ruthy's lovely complexion was no more. It had been replaced by thousands of red spots. I tried to speak, but nothing would come out.

"Don't worry, I can fix this," Ruthy's mother said. She scurried away like a crab, not really forward, more sideways, looking back as if half expecting me to leg it. I know I begin to sound like that fellow Flashman from that silly book but damn it, it was outrageous. I recalled how the Mongols tossed the bodies of their plague victims at the city of Caffa on the Black Sea (1346); Ruthy would have been an early toss. I had begun to suggest to Ruthy that perhaps we should leave it for a week or two, as we could always sit at home and hold hands, when her mother reappeared.

"We will just apply a little of this and you'll see, good as new. She's like me, we both get these nasty outbreaks when we are nervous but they don't last."

The mother started spreading Clearasil on her daughter's face with a vigor born of desperation. To that she added something called Aconomel, which brought a heady sort of hospital smell as in a busy operating room. After a few minutes, the woman said, "We're ready."

It was if I were staring at a plastic replica of Ruth, a very shiny replica. She was fully encased in the two substances liberally applied. She couldn't seem to breathe through her nose at all and was making a kind of bassoon noise through her mouth.

"Perfect!" her mother shouted.

Ruthy looked at me with pleading eyes. We had to get out of there.

"Shoosh " said Ruth, which I took to be an agreement of some sort, and we were off leaving a freely perspiring Mrs. Hallry to, no doubt, have a huge dollop of Polish brandy, which she had told me, was just for special occasions. The next thing I know I was sitting in the Gardens parking lot. I was determined to talk Ruthy out of going to the game for all our sakes. Still, sitting there in the soft light in a corner of the lot, she didn't look that bad, especially since she was stroking my trembling leg. So we passed through the turnstiles on our way to our seats in the reds. As her mother fussed with her face, Ruthy was wearing her raincoat. When she removed it in the company box, she revealed a puce and purple number that would have drawn comment at a Mafia wedding. The unsuspecting patrons of the hockey game that long ago night were used to seeing the occasional strange and wonderful vision, after all hockey brought out the visually strange and wonderful in a usually very boring land of people, for Canadians like their meat and potatoes with the occasional veg but were not opposed to a brief nod to other cultures as long as they could scurry home for the 11 o'clock news. The first hint of something wrong was when the man selling programs started to cross himself but I brushed it off as another example of taking too many Slavic types from the nearby refugee camps.

As I watched Tim Horton and Dick Duff fly past us in the warmup, I remembered the announcement the week before that this game would be the first one broadcast in colour on television. This was brought to my attention in a number of ways. First the heat was much higher than normal, brought on, I saw, by the five new banks of lights set up for the new technology. In fact many people were wearing sunglasses. Second, my date began to look as if she was a melting candle. I cocked a wary eye around me, only to confirm the worst. Even the players seemed to be going out of their way to have a look at us. Ruthy seemed oblivious to the unwanted attention and was actually waving to the players and they were waving back, the cheeky beggars. Suddenly it dawned on me that everyone I knew was there. All my friends were using their parent's tickets, like me. I now took in the full Technicolor luridness of Ruthy's face. There were eruptions everywhere. Whiteheads and pustules were rampant and with the extra light, the Gardens felt like a dermatologists' convention with 15,000 drooling doctors looking at my date.

I throw myself at your mercy. What could I do? Oh, I know, not all of the crowd was looking at us, but to a boy of 16, it seemed that way. What had not bothered me about her before now loomed into view. Her choice of clothing was beyond garish and her face was beginning to take on a new hue, a brighter one. Some fool acquaintance beside our aisle pretended to be unable to look at her directly and so was using a mirror, I would have loved to sort him out. Instead, the courage of the Clarkes fizzled in my breast and I felt the hand of a coward grabbing at my heart.

We Clarkes are in the Doomsday Book as part of the Conqueror's bunch, late of Normandy. It is also said we helped cart William's body from his place of death at Mantes in the summer of 1087. His passing, as everyone knows, happened when his horse reared and he being a touch overweight, the pommel of his saddle tore into his bowels, making for an uncomfortable death. It wasn't our fault that some idiot put the great leader into a smallish casket, and how was my ancestor L'clarke to know that the next day would be extremely hot? Any student of rudimentary physics could have predicted the outcome. So when the coffin exploded the following day about 1:30 p.m. who do you think Rufus and his lot went after when we were just trying to help?

However those days are gone and the Clarke seed has thinned out, till it now produces poor wretches like me.

What happened next I would do anything to reverse. Ruthy, can you ever forgive me? There were so many other things I could have done. I could have simply said I was ill and could we leave please, or this game is so boring, let's go and have a dinner. In fact anything would have been preferable to what really happened. I can still see her face full of hope, knowing something was wrong, trying her best in the midst of everything foreign. As the first period ended, I shot to my feet, braying, "Would you care for refreshments?"

"Yes, please," she said, as the soft cream from her forehead oozed over her brow.

"Perhaps you could hand me my coat as it is chilly," I said.

She gave it to me. She wanted to come with me, I could tell, but I waved her off and started down the stairs towards the exit. I had to turn back as I reached the floor of the Gardens and pass beneath her. I retain the horrible image of her look to this day, the look of a trapped animal about to be euthanized. I waved brightly. There was still time to turn back. Then I saw Atkinson, the little swine, grinning down from his seat behind us.

"Where did you find the dog, Clarke? " he shouted to an appreciative roar from the friends around him.

That was all it took. I shot through the doors of the Gardens, ran to the car and in a trice was home watching the game in the comfort of the family rec. room. I got a Carling Red Cap from the fridge and settled onto the couch as the second period got under way. It wasn't hard to spot my erstwhile date — occasionally there would be a face-off just below our seats and a purple image of Ruthy would emerge. There she was with three empty seats, staring over the exit wall, no doubt praying for my return. Watching that gave me my first spasm of doubt. Perhaps I had been slightly rash. Then I thought hopefully that a jury of my peers would agree with the steps I had taken. On the other hand what must poor Ruthy have been going through, alone and not looking her best with no money nor car nor date to see her home? As these facts hit home, I began to stir uneasily. Perhaps I should return to the rink and rescue her. Sadly I followed the Ancient Mariner down the road of deep regret. I changed the channel and tried to forget. My curiosity made me return to the game. By the third period she had gone. There were four empty seats staring back at me as the proof of my shame. I realized I had done something truly dreadful and there would be a price exacted, as there always is.

The next day the calls started coming in as the news spread from those near us at the Gardens. To certain of my friends I was a hero for not putting up with an untenable position but there was shock and disbelief from many, many others. One girl called me the cruelest man since Richard the Third.

Education can limit one to the shallow ramblings of an idiotic teacher claiming to be an historian. One needs to research one's subject thoroughly for one's self. Dear Richard only murdered the two princes, and even that is suspect, although they did find some bones in the tower recently, but he was not a terrible king by any means. However history is written by the winners, in this case, the Tudors. Sir Thomas More was commissioned to write a history of the War of the Roses by Henry the Seventh and presented it to his son, Henry the Eighth. More was no idiot, so he painted Richard with an ugly brush. More simply left him as "hunchbacked and hated , he had but a short reign" This no doubt put a smile on Henry's handsome face, who bestowed many honours on More. He would not be the first historian to know his audience. Still More had a torture chamber in his house for religious shirkers, so he was not so pleasant himself, but because Henry beheaded him for his objections to his wedding of Anne, history has been kind to him.

Even this might not have doomed Richard to the depths of history had it not been for our friend Shakespeare, who used More's book to create the famous play that is almost mandatory at every summer Shakespearean Festival.

However Stalin was indisputably a true monster having liquidated 30 million or so of his own people in the Ukraine and Georgia with the collective farms disaster . His slaughter in the late 30's of the officer corps of the Red Army gave Hitler the encouragement and after Finland's heroic defense, to attack Russia and open up a second front.

Where was I? Oh, yes, people calling me a monster, only a few, well, more than a few. I hardened myself for the recriminations but it died down fairly quickly. After all, who really knew Ruthy? But the stain on my soul remained. The summer was over so there was no reason to go to the cricket club for the rest of that year. I heard later that Ruthy had left and I never found out where she went or whether she kept up her skating. I did hear years later that she would not blame me for that night, only herself. What a girl.

Before you get all high and mighty about what I did, let me remind you that I owned up to it. How many of you would have swept it under the rug? No, I came clean and that has to count for something. I know I sound like that Alfie chap from the movie, but this isn't a movie and I told the truth.

CHAPTER 3

(Robert's inglorious start at school. He described this time as "his troubled period," but one can see that it was here, even at so young an age, that he began to acquire his awful reputation. We think one will see that Robert had many troubled periods throughout his life. Ed.)

To really understand what happened to me we have to travel back to my early schooling, and when I look back, it is a wonder I turned out as well as I did. At the age of four, off I went to Mrs. Crow's Nursery School and oh, how I loved it. I have forgotten the name of the game where you remove a chair after each verse of music — I triumphed at it. The girls played as well, but we just pushed them off their seats when the music stopped. So it would end up with, say, four boys and three seats, with each of us eyeing the other. Mrs. Crow seemed to encourage us the harder and more vicious we became. She also had a ponderous bosom to which all boys loved to be clutched. If one of us were hurt, she would rush to his assistance, pick him up and thrust him between her two pillars of Hercules, where she would rub him around for a while. I didn't know why I liked it so much but there was no mistaking that I did.

The nursery school was a little house on Summerhill Road near Chorley Park, where we children were allowed at lunch to watch the men trying to sign up for the Korean War. The lines of men wearing their leftover khaki from the last war five years past snaked through the neighbourhood. My first memory of looking up a girl's skirt is at the nursery school. Mrs. Crow didn't seem to mind — she would just cuff Russell or me if we were caught — but the girls did. Russell, my best friend in 1950, and I would discuss for hours how was it that if girls didn't want us to look up their dresses they still wore cute little plaid skirts that were very short, and then twirled in them, which made them almost nonexistent. It was the first time I used the excuse "I couldn't help myself" when I was caught for the fourth time in one afternoon staring up a skirt. I wasn't caught by a teacher, but by the object of my passion, the girl herself.

Why try to make me crazy in the first place? It was the same thing when I was older: no meant yes. Oh, yes, it did, because no girl wanted to be known as someone who ever said yes and yet if you persisted she would make you promise not to tell and then open her treasure to you. It seems now like such a waste, but that's the way it was. It was so much fun to watch (and occasionally participate) later on in the mid-1960s as those same girls paraded around in the buff and made love with such abandon.

Back to Mrs. Crow's. It is a strange world, isn't it, because many years later I managed to sleep with Mrs. Crow's granddaughter at her cottage quite by chance. I had met her at a dock party and after a few Pat Boone songs she was mine. Her last name wasn't Crow, and she told me she was staying at her grandmother's. In the morning I almost dropped dead when I realized who she was, but the elderly Mrs. Crow just smiled and walked away.

She and the school were a Rosedale tradition. It was where I first heard certain words that remain part of my lexicon today. I remember it started with Betty falling (pushed, more like it) and Mrs. Crow attending to it, saying, "Did you hurt your go-go, Betty, dear?" What did this mean, go-go? I asked my amused sister, who had attended the same school nine years earlier and remembered all of Mrs. Crow's ways. She drew me a sketch in her Hilary cahier showing a girl's vagina. "That's a go-go?" I asked. "Correct," replied my sister Jane, "And yours is called Sebastian." This gave me food for thought. To the hilarity of the neighbours, I took to the streets yelling, "Betty hurt her go-go, but Sebastian is all right."

Mrs. Crow also is responsible for naming bowel movements as "going big," as in "Does anyone have to go big before we have lunch, children?" To this day I love embarrassing my 55-year-old brother by enquiring whether he has to go big and wondering how his Sebastian is. Who Sebastian was in Mrs. Crow's life we never discovered. After Mrs. Crow's we moved as a group to Whitney School, above the tracks in Moore Park, for kindergarten.

I love history in general, but there is something truly wonderful about medieval England because so much was going on that would change the world or set in play future events. For instance, the Black Death first visited England in 1348 and 1349. Not content with that it returned in 1361, 1368, 1374, 1379 and 1390. Looking back upon my two years at Whitney School, I am sure there are a few retired teachers who mark 1951 and 1952 as their years of the plague. I was, I think, never a bad boy as much as a naughty one, an inquisitive six-year-old let loose in a large school with no minute-by-minute control such as in nursery school. No Mrs. Crow scanning her charges for horseplay or injury. My sister would walk me over the train tracks to the bottom of Summerhill Road below the school and leave me to catch the Mount Pleasant bus to Havergal College. As I walked up towards the looming school, I was on my own.

There was a hill on the school property that was for girls only. If a girl you were chasing in order to see up her skirt made it to the hill, you could not follow. Where's the fairness in that? This was one of many lessons learned in those early years: the unfairness of life and the cunning it would take to circumvent the inequities.

Ah, yes, the hill. Since most of the girls in my class were graduates of Mrs. Crow's and who remembered little Robert Clarke only too well, there was no sanctuary from their abuse once they had made it to the hill. Shouts of "How's your Sebastian?" would bring quizzical looks from the uninitiated amongst the baying boys at the bottom of the hill. This was tantamount to pouring hot oil from the parapets on the soldiers below.

History tells us many things, as my father would say endlessly. He was what could be called an amateur historian, and he studied assiduously throughout his life. From the living room one could hear the sounds of Father reading: "Aha!" or "The fool," and "I knew it." It was sometimes uncomfortable for my sister and me, as Father expected us to keep up with him and might be stunned that we had not read Lord Robert's *My Years in India, 1888-98*. It often led to privations. When the roast had been served and the word was out there might be second helpings, Father would give us that gimlet eye of his and ask, "What is considered Napoleon's last great victory?" and if you didn't quickly say, "Austerlitz," there was no more for you. My sister did well in the early goings and I had to be content with trying to steal scraps, as I was especially partial to the crispy skin of the well-done outside of the roast beef.

This had its own hazards, for Father was adroit at slicing through the air with the carving knife, turning it over at the last moment so only the blunt side hit my thieving hand. This gave great delight to my sister and the vapours to my fluttering mother, plus, blunt or not, it still bloody well hurt. Under the circumstances I fast became an amateur historian too, for at that age one is always hungry. I soon impressed Father with obscure facts from the Boy's Own, which arrived from the U.K. every month, for I had discovered that if one could steer

Father onto the subject you wanted, he might not ask you the questions that he originally had in mind.

"King Richard had 3,000 hostages slaughtered before the walls of Acre in order to speed up the surrender of the city," I ventured quickly when I realized a glazed ham with pineapples and maraschino cherries was about to be served. Father, though pleased, was no fool and shot back, "Who was Richard's father?"

"Henry the Second," I parried.

He was smiling broadly. He asked what I knew would be my last question, "And what was his last name?"

"Plantagenet."

"Correct!" bellowed my father, "Correct!"

My sister sat mutely near my mother, trying to give me what she called her death-ray gaze. It was not my fault she hadn't noticed the book Father had been reading for over a week, about the life of Saladin and the infidels. All I did was realize that Father's mind would probably be stockpiling facts about King Richard's crusades and Saladin's response. Richard was to my mind a hero, as we had grown up on Robin Hood stories which, while Robin probably didn't exist, certainly contained oodles about King Richard, most of it untrue. For a start he spoke French, not English, was bisexual and rarely spent time in England during his 10-year reign. He also nearly bankrupted the country with his bloody crusades and then truly ruined England when the country had to ransom its king from Leopold of Austria for 100,000 silver crowns. He didn't even think of himself as English — rather, like his father, he believed he was Norman. So when he died by an arrow from a crossbow at the age of 41 near Chalus, France, he was disemboweled, salted and buried in Northern France. Nevertheless I wanted to believe that Richard was the Lion Heart of TV Robin Hood fame and that his brother, Prince John, would get his just deserts. He did in a swamp-like field near Windsor called Runnymede.

At kindergarten I first discovered the whisper of silk stockings (probably nylon) and the effect that they would have on me for the rest of my life. Miss Peacock was our teacher and I would guess now, all of 23 or 24 years old, blonde and gorgeous. She did not look or smell like our mothers or sisters.

Being very small in comparison to our elders gave us an odd outlook on life. All was seen from a dog's point of view: large at the bottom, disappearing near the top. When someone older leaned down towards us, it was as if something was rushing at us, inspecting and finding us wanting. Miss Peacock, on the other hand, would gently take our hands as she sat down in one of our undersized chairs, speaking softly, with a wonderful scent that clung to her. I loved Miss Peacock as only the very young can love, deeply and without reservation. I never knew blonde could be as blonde as the hair with little wisps that fell forward before her perfect ears. When she turned her head the wisps soothed the air around her and then settled slightly after she did.

My favourite time was just after lunch, when Miss Peacock would take a book from her bureau and ask us to sit down in front of her reading chair and listen to a story. The girls would seat themselves closest to the teacher whilst the boys would be expected to ring the girls on the outer edges. I did not get that memo. Instead I waded into the girls with the fervor of a crusader trying to get into the gates of Jerusalem. I remember the girls taking extreme umbrage, for they loved her too, but when we had all settled and Miss Peacock had done the class count, she would take her seat. If I was in the front row, she had to sit down right in front of me.

I have to explain a bit. My friend Russell, while we were gasping for breath a few days before, having chased some wretched but quick girls up the hill, imparted to me the knowledge that, on the front end of girls, in fact at the go-go, there was a dark cave. The world reeled. I could hardly credit this testimony. "How do you know this?" I inquired, grabbing his arm and twisting. Torture was, as the Syrians have been telling us for years, the fast way to the truth or at least a confession of some sort.

"'Struth," he gurgled as I attached my other hand to his throat. I loosened my grip slightly.

Russell swore he had seen his mother's dark cave in the reflection of her dressing table mirror whilst hanging from a well-situated vine on the outside of his family's house. There was some believability in his strangled words, as we had spent many a happy hour nestled in the ivy at his house, trying to catch a glimpse of his mother's hangers. He had always claimed that his mother's turned up while our mothers' sagged from suckling and childbirth. The jury was not convinced, as she never seemed comfortable enough to disrobe while two or three of us sat at our perch in the trellis. Looking back, perhaps Russell's mother was wary of showing herself because of the fogging on the window from our anticipating mouths.

Russell now said he had seen his mother and not only did her breasts go up, but she had something nasty between her legs. To be fair we had seen the odd "gash" on a girl or two but the actual GO-GO seemed astringent and uninteresting, made only for "Rinky Tinky", while their cute little bums seemed far more interesting. Russell described it as hairy spider that seemed to be hurt or something, for there was an angry pink seam in the middle. The world began to swim as I sat down at the bottom of the hill. A well-thrown stone caught my knee as the dreadful Jennifer began to get her range. I barely looked up.

"This means Miss Peacock may have one too," I pondered as another stone shot past my ear.

"I suppose so," replied Russell, taking one in the stomach, "I wonder if it hurts her," he added somberly.

So the stage was set for my obsession to be close to Mrs. Peacock's legs during her afternoon readings. Week after week

I would sit right in front of her, straining to get a glimpse of her inner thigh as she crossed and uncrossed her legs, but something else happened: I became aware of the whisper of her stockings. While I had to still maintain my place in the front row, I could rest my eyes and listen to the siren song of a woman's legs whispering to a little boy of greater things.

However as I have done many times since, I overplayed my hand. This will not surprise relatives or teachers, although if there were not people like us, there would be no stories to tell. It is not as if we want to go too far or even if we know where too far really is, as the boundaries seem to move about with great alacrity. It is like picking on people with Tourette's syndrome — they can't help it. Enjoy the performance and leave them alone.

Speaking of Tourette's syndrome I recall going to a client meeting in New York in my twenties where a lovely account girl was showing, by way of charts, what the agency planned for that year's advertising campaign. The company being pitched was family owned and normally run by the two sons of the honorary chairman, but this time the chairman had decided to see for himself what the new campaign would consist of. It quickly became apparent why he was not involved in the day to day workings of the company. He had not been sitting long before odd noises began to be heard from the distinguished gentleman.

"Holy fuck!" he bellowed at the poor woman trying to give a breakdown of the demographics the campaign aimed for. This outburst brought a few smiles from the rest of us, but when we realized that the sons were sitting there stony-faced we wiped our grins off fast.

"Burp, burp and a fart," he continued happily, as a few of us choked down the urge to giggle. I am not good at containing myself in these sorts of situation. I often look at the wealthy and say to myself, "Now there go people who did NOT giggle at inappropriate moments".

The president of the advertising agency had begun to perspire freely as several of his cohorts played with ties, while others stared at their feet which had suddenly become terribly interesting. I began to write gibberish on my note-pad in a desperate effort to contain myself. I should have excused myself and left, for I knew I could not take much more and I had a long history of creating an uproar at inappropriate times. "What's she wearing underneath?" he inquired of one of his statue-like sons in his booming voice.

I was done. Air began to escape from my pressed lips and the agency guys looked on with clinical interest at a career suicide. I began to turn a new and rather dangerous shade of purple.

"Great tits," said the man and with that I slid onto the floor in a paroxysm of laughter.

I have to give the agency boss credit. He tried to perform CPR and the kiss of life on me in a desperate pretense at bringing a heart attack victim back to life. Alas there could be no cover-up and I was drummed out of that particular agency. Kind hands led the chairman away as he shouted: "It's not over. It's not over, goddammit, I paid to see those horns."

But you see what I mean. No one was angry with the old chairman, who was suffering with a sad malady (although he looked pretty happy to me), just at people like me who couldn't contain themselves. The last words I heard from the chairman as they escorted him out was, "That was fun," and it was.

In the case of Miss Peacock, it was simply that I never broke my concentration from her lovely stockinged legs. If once in awhile I had looked up at her face or murmured quietly like the others, I might have gone unnoticed. Instead I stared at the hem of her dress without let-up. We had a cat at home in those days called Biscuit, who was a tough tomcat and ruled the neighbourhood like a dictator. Fully half of the young cats one saw had somewhat the same colouring as Biscuit, no doubt from his nightly sojourns. He seemed to treat all the cats well, as long as they recognized his standing and obeyed. Father thought the name Biscuit made him sound a bit of a pansy, and once mentioned that point of view. However, Mother stopped fluttering long enough to fix Father with a look that reminded me and no doubt him of an annoyed Amazon about to put a poisoned arrow on the string of her bow. Thus no more was said about the name, for she had named Biscuit after a long dead cat who was the best friend of an only child — her.

The reason I mentioned our cat was simply to point out that I had often taken note of how hunting was at his core. Many of Biscuit's fellow cats were content to eat bonbons, followed by a kindly stroking before an early night. Not our cat. Out all night, rested all day.

I saw him many times crawling into a position and remaining frozen for hours. The errant feathers and half-eaten rodents all over the back garden were proof of his success. Mother would often spot the cat focused on a hole in the garage wall down by the bottom of the garden. She would surge into action, telling the maid to see that the cat not hurt a bird or whatnot. Elizabeth our Austrian maid (because no one could be German yet) would take the glass jar that she kept for the milk money, haul back and throw jar and contents at the cat, usually catching him in the short ribs. Elizabeth had eaten many cats on her trek across war-torn Eastern Europe and had no interest in Biscuit's welfare. The cat never moved, not even a raised eyebrow toward the cat-eater. This is how I approached Miss Peacock's stockings.

I stared straight at the firmness of her calves tapering north to the knees with their promise of what lay ahead. They were pressed together at all times, and while the rest of Miss Peacock breathed, they did not. Old people are warned against too much leg-crossing as it results in unhappiness for all the veins concerned, but in young Miss Peacock there was no such worry. It troubles me now to think that what was a cathedral of young beauty is now very likely dust or at the least, as Henry the Eighth said on his wedding night to Catharine Parr, the last of his eight wives, "I am a mountain of corruption."

And so day after day I gaped during story hour at the tightly placed knees, looking for the cave. It was odd Russell didn't particularly care for the delights of the upper stocking scenario. Lacking imagination, he only wanted the sight of flesh, and generally just his mother's.

If Henry the Fifth had thought like that, Agincourt would have been a different kettle of fish. On that day almost 600 years ago, he imagined that 6,000 men sick with dysentery, English and Welsh with longbows that they had been trained to use since their youth, could win against 36,000 French. From that imagination sprang one of the greatest routs in history, with only a few hundred English casualties and the flower of France knighthood gone.

It is no doubt a credit to Miss Peacock's patience that she allowed this behaviour of mine to linger on as long as it did, and even then I must point elsewhere for my undoing. Into the singsong lullaby of Miss Peacock's stockings came the visage of that deadly stone-thrower, Jennifer. She was a freckled fiend with a throwing arm that made the Society of Goliaths quail whenever she was mentioned. I blamed Canada's lax immigration laws for the fact that she and her family had washed up upon our beach from Scotland. I rather thought that some sort of mutiny must have taken place by the more sensible types on board some previously happy ship and the MacDonnells had been put overboard with every hope of them drowning. Sadly no. Her father worked as a gardener, of whom it was said he so frightened his employer, a retired general who had once run Canada's most dangerous prison, that he allowed the tribe of eleven MacDonnell cannibals to move into his mansion, forcing the school board to allow Jennifer to attend the nearby Whitney. I know Miss Peacock must have felt slightly uncomfortable with my rapt attention to her knees and the insipid way I had of licking my lips, but we did not need Jennifer sticking her oar into our story hour and forcing dear Miss Peacock to see finally what she had always felt.

"Miss Peacock! Och, Miss Peacock!" she cried one day.

Miss Peacock raised the bluest of eyes in her direction. Jennifer normally sat at the back of the class mumbling to herself; all kinds of incantations could be heard in some forgotten tongue. Jennifer had no friends of any sex and brooded mightily most of the time. So now to have her put a few words together was dumbfounding. We, along with Miss Peacock, turned in her freckled direction.

"Och, wooman, yaaa have a parve thar in wee Robert," she said.

There are a lot of subjects that puzzle twenty-one kindergarten children. How we came to be there, for instance. Or why Russell's mother's breasts went up. But in this case we settled back for a translation. None came. Today Miss Peacock would simply have referred her to the upstairs ESL class, two doors down from the grief counsellor, but those great strides had not as yet been contemplated.

"Eh?" said Miss Peacock. Her question was followed by a number of sounds from Jennifer not unlike a steam engine having started climbing too steep a grade and found itself wanting: "Och, noooo, och mon," etc.

The Toronto School Board was well known for dealing with all of God's children and their speech impediments, as well as a great number of suspect cultures from around the globe. The board's book Questionable Children was the stuff of much midnight reading amongst the intelligentsia concerned for little innocents still in their states of grace. Miss Peacock began to rifle through a well-thumbed QC, but all was silent on "Scottish fecund families." It went from warning male teachers to avoid children who practiced the "scissor kick" at swimming classes because there was every chance that when cornered, said children would scissor-kick male teachers in the goolies, to "scouser," a native of Liverpool. Eventually she discovered that Jennifer was calling me a pervert for sitting so close to Miss. Peacock's knees.

To be fair, Jennifer had only triggered what had already been in Miss Peacock's mind, a certain uncomfortable feeling of being gazed at a little too hard by me. I thus joined the ranks of the untouchables. Unfortunately there were not many of us, so I couldn't hide, but I contented myself with the knowledge that Julius Caesar had borne a lousy reputation through most of his life and had still succeeded. The rumour was that as a teenaged boy, Caesar had been buggered repeatedly by Nicomedes, who was king of what is now Turkey (Bithynia). In fact Nicomedes was said to have taken his virginity. It was probably the cause of his never-ending need to sleep with all his friend's wives, even Servilia, the mother of his future assassin, Brutus. Not content with that, Servilia was said to have brought Tertia, her daughter, to Caesar's bed, and she was married to Cassius. I am always amused that each generation thinks it is breaking new ground in the sex department when really it is simply following well-worn paths from history. As for me, I have tried in my heart to blame my future exploits as a Lothario as some sort of revenge on Miss Peacock's class and the dreadful Jennifer, but if I am honest, I was, as my father pointed out many times, a little strange to begin with.

The untouchables were not allowed to go outside at recess. No, we sat in the library and stared at picture books, as we had not started to read for ourselves yet. Even the poor teacher who was in charge of us, Mr. Reid, was an untouchable: he stuttered. The only way he could impart knowledge was by singing everything he was trying to get across. Since he couldn't carry a tune, the untouchable class took on the sound of an unamused cat being swung by its tail.

I gather he was inspired by Tiberius Claudius Caesar, who, following the murder of his nephew Caligula in 41 AD, became emperor. Known not only for his survival abilities but also for his terrible stutter, he still managed to rule for thirteen years. He enlarged the empire by annexing Britain, Mauritania and Thrace until finally being poisoned by his fourth wife, Agrippina, in 54 AD. Mr. Reid had an odd way of trying to keep time while singing, by adding nonsense phrases during his efforts. When he came to our inaugural recess detention, he opened the door and sang, "Tra la, my name is Mr. Reid, boom boom."

I didn't mind much, although it gave me a bit of a start. The effect on others, especially Peter John, was more deleterious. By any measure he was an appalling child. Having a Christian name as one's last name meant teasing and harassment from a fairly large contingent led by Jennifer, who was equally troubled by the fact he was an only child and clearly not a Catholic. He also had the Boils of Job. His face and what body we could see was alive with what looked like a sort of mild plague. All this and a nervous condition shot him into the air, doing a not bad pike with a twist when the singing, stuttering Mr. Reid threw open the door to the library that first morning.

We also had a schoolmate named Rebecca who refused to look in the direction of the person addressing her, so much so other kids would run around her as she looked away, making her spin and then collapse. Poor girl, she could not hide on the hill as the other girls refused to have her up there. At the door opening, her head seem to rotate fully twice. There was another boy in the detention who sobbed constantly. For the only time in my life, I appeared the most normal and civilized person in the room.

"RRRRRRRRRRRRRRRRRRRRRRRRRR," Mr. Reid began. "RRRROOOOOOOOOOBBB," he tried again, all for naught. I was tempted to shout, "Sing it, sir," but the rumour was he could became quite unhinged if a child suggested that, so I let him get on with it.

"Tra lee, Robert, boom boom, would you take attendance, please, fa la!" he got out, then sat down exhausted.

I looked over at Peter John, who had reacquired his seat, then at Rebecca, now showing a lovely view of her spinal column, and merely heard the sobbing boy. "All present, sir," I said, trying not to laugh.

And so it went with the untouchables, week after week. Well, one makes do as best one can under any circumstances. What must it have been like in the Black Hole of Calcutta, a small jail cell made for ten containing 143 British prisoners following the capture of Calcutta by the Nawab of Bengal in June 1756. Only 23 survived. I meant to be one of the survivors of the untouchables.

We were allowed to attend our normal classes the rest of the time but it was not as if anyone had forgotten my sins, so I sat way at the back, straining even to hear the story, much less see the delicious Miss Peacock. She, I must say, had become rather distant and cold toward me and not for the last time did I ponder life's unfairness. There I was minding my own business, sitting in the front row, listening to her story. OK, so I was also trying to look up her skirt. Here lies the first inequity: she was wearing a skirt, and I was sitting in the front row. Where else would I look as a normal six-year-old boy? Medically my neck could not take the strain of looking straight up at her face. Second, Becky, who sat beside me in the first row, also had to look at Miss Peacock's knees, and nothing was ever said about that. Girls were never called out on things like that; anything evil, hang the boy. It really is a miracle that I have turned out as well as I have. I should be part of some 50's Kindergarten "Truth and Reconciliation" program today receiving thousands for what I was put through. Bah. I was just left to soldier on.

Russell would still play with me, but only away from Whitney School. I don't blame him really, and he remained my closest friend until he moved away two years later. After that first year Miss Peacock left the school to travel, but many of the awful girls on the hill blamed me for her departure. Phooey! She left, I chose to believe, because she felt terrible about my treatment, and couldn't face her true love any longer. I still thought we might be an item some day if she could bear the wait. This thinking, which I shared with my classmates, brought nothing but fury from the hill, but who cared anyway, for I was headed to Grade One.

I will not bore you with the full extent of Grade One; here, however, are the salient points.

My teacher Miss Somebody, which shows how little I cared for her, was not attractive. She only shaved to just below her knees, and the effect was not pleasant. It looked like illegal farming had taken place, combined with some sort of burn off, while north of the knee was a thick rainforest not yet claimed by the farmers in the south. The first word in spelling taught to me in Grade One was "farm" and then "goat." Literacy was the greatest gift imparted to me by Whitney School, and to that nameless but hirsute teacher, I remain grateful.

I became more popular that year; I don't know why, but the girls seemed to relent in their dislike of me. I even heard one girl refer to me as "cute as a button," although upon spotting me screamed, "Yuck, it's Robert," and ran for the hill. However, I had gleaned my first compliment from the fairer sex, and it gave me the strut that I carry to this day.

CHAPTER 4

(Crescent School looms before Clarke....Matron and the Masters, boarding school at seven. Ed)

Not long ago, propped up by the bar at my club, meditating on the late autumn of my life, I realized with that old but not forgotten rush of warmth to my trousers that I had at one time or another slept with every woman sitting in the club dining room. I tripped a passing waiter to tell him of this. I pressed money into his hand, flaunting club rules, but hang the bloody rules, for that man amongst men saw as I did: I have lived a full and colourful life. I thought of my father, all that he had taught me old chap and how fond I was of him. However I am also reminded that he sent me off to his old boarding school as the youngest boarder in the school's history for Grade 2.

Talk about indulgences from the church — think of what the old salmon had to go through to have me shut away at the Crescent School, as that place is still called. I take it from my sister Jane that Mater and Pater's marriage was going through a tricky patch at that time and they needed a round-the-world cruise to recover, so I, a boy of seven, stood at the gates of private school and the prospect of living in.

Matron was the first to notice me at the main school doors and beckoned to me from the nearby window. My Uncle Tony, who was really my godfather, had dropped me off. Tony Cottrell had been my father's best friend in the army, and though they started together as corporals in the infantry, Tony had soon been seconded to the artillery because of his superb math skills. He returned home a major, almost totally deaf from the guns. Father gave him a job at Clarke Furniture, running scheduling and delivery, aspects requiring Tony's analytical mind. Since Mother and Father were already on the cruise, Uncle Tony was given the job of delivering the package, namely me. He had found civilian life hard, at least anything away from his math and paperwork, and as a result became adept at writing long and instructive letters, thus avoiding the embarrassment of shouting loudly and in confined spaces "What?" and "Say again."

Such was the case as we pulled up to the front doors of my new school. He had prepared one of his flowery explanations on his own stationery with green ink (he enjoyed reading Oscar Wilde). He shook my hand, gave me the letter marked "The Headmaster," indicated the ten-foot-tall doors and bid me adieu. I stood beside my trunk and watched the retreating image of my godfather's car going down the stone driveway and began to cry. It was a great lesson in life learned earlier than most. Just because you cry doesn't mean anyone is going to help you. It's not like home. No one is coming. After a while I stopped crying and looked around at the surroundings, and noticed it was lovely.

There was a huge pile of a castle surrounded by hills and green playing fields as far as I could see. I sat down on my trunk and looked at the big grey school. My father had attended Crescent and now sat on the board of governors, with the particular duty of raising money for this impoverished seat of highly specialized teaching. That commitment and the annual fees were the price my father paid to get the youngest boarder in the school's history into a dorm. After some time, the great doors opened and there stood a startling replica of Queen Victoria, who, if I was not mistaken, had been dead for fifty odd years. Father had a large picture of the monarch over the mantle in our living room, so I was well aware of her visage. The dead queen held out her hand, saying, "Welcome to the Crescent School."

I learned later that the older staff always referred to the school with the formal "the" as a nod to some anachronism. The monarch continued, "I am Miss Payne. Please refer to me as Matron. And you are…?" raising her prominent eyebrows.

Uncle Tony, like my father, could not stand lateness of any sort and had always considered it a thrashing offense. As a consequence, we had arrived at the school fully an hour early. Uncle Tony said it was his first visit to the school and he wished to leave time in case we missed it. That hardly seemed likely, as it was some five miles outside Toronto and the only landmark for miles around. Having arrived early, we doubled back a mile or so to find a restaurant, where my uncle fed me buttered toast and endless amounts of Canada Dry ginger ale.

Like many men of his generation Uncle Tony felt that it was a matter of patriotism for Canadians to drink that particular brand to fight the creeping Americanism of the nefarious Coke. Canada Dry had been founded north of Toronto at the forks of the Credit River. It was owned by the Maclachlin family, made famous by Sam Maclachlin, the inventor of the Buick car and Oshawa's most famous resident. Sadly, like the Buick, Canada Dry's ownership soon made its way south to America.

The point I'm trying to make is I was full of ginger ale and now wanted the WC badly, but did not have the where with all to ask the Queen where it was. So there I stood, frozen by the question. I had as a matter of fact been tested before for incontinence, as would any man or beast faced with Dr. Withrow's sermons at St. Paul's Church on Bloor Street.

"God's teeth," my father would murmur under his breath, having glanced at his watch while seated in the Clarke pew at Sunday service; the good doctor had yet to reach the fullness of his weekly sermon and close to 30 minutes had gone by. By fullness he meant getting within sight of the point of the lecture, usually signaled by a deepening hue starting at the priest's neck and heading towards the broken veins of his cheeks. No such colour had as yet appeared. What upset father and the other sides-men as much as the boredom, was the congregation would use the offertory hymn to bolt in search of bladder relief, thus making the collection during the hymn less than could have been expected had it been a short pithy sermon.

Many elderly types could be seen leaving both wet and wretched, flinging embittered glances at the good doctor. So I well understood the need for waiting before going. However what was new to me was terror and Mr. Prig. For as I was looking at Miss Payne and she looking at me, I was suddenly manhandled from behind.

"Shall I have to flog some manners into you, boy, speak to Matron!" Mr. Prig spat out. This was not a bit like being afraid of one's father, as there was underlying love there, not here. It was clear: The rules had changed and there would be no mitigating circumstances, no family pity from my mother or the usual flock of maiden aunts, no, I could be flogged just because this man felt like it. That was essentially the lay of the land for the rest of my formal schooling, although I couldn't have imagined it that day. To my shame the Canada Dry chose this moment to force my frightened bladder to let go and it did so with a vengeance. Out the bottom of my Eaton's short trousers and past my knees came a yellow Niagara, shooting down my grey high socks and pooling for a moment on my shiny black oxfords before spreading onto the gravel driveway.

"He's a beast, Miss Payne, a beast of the field!" Mr. Prig shouted at the top of his lungs with a plummy English accent. I burst into tears, which only brought renewed outrage from Mr. Prig.

"Hold him, Matron, whilst I visit the forest and retrieve a cane, because we should start as we mean to go on, eh, Matron?"

"Waaaaaaaaaaaaaaaa," I added.

"Boy, I will slap you silly if you don't stop that caterwauling now, DO YOU HEAR, BOY??

More urine shot from my nether regions as the master, for that was what I learned Mr. Prig and his colleagues were referred to as, started to dance with rage. Now I was truly frightened. Miss Payne at last put a stop to it.

"He has yet to check in, Mr. Prig. You'll have your chance to abuse him at a later date, but right now he is mine," she said and marched me into the school, taking my hand as we went. Grateful for any respite from Mr. Prig, I readily went along.

The world of an English boys' school greeted me that day and it was a feeling I shall never forget. We paused as we entered a huge rotunda with hallways drifting off in all directions and the scent of a hundred boys. Doors opened and shut with the comings and goings of black-caped masters and green-jacketed boys, with a sprinkling of servants and female secretaries. In spite of my wet clothes and obvious embarrassment, there was something about it — elitism, an honour, I am not sure, but I felt that I belonged there and it became my real home for the next five years.

Crescent School had been set up, according to all the stories, by a nice man called Mr. James in 1913 as a smaller boys' school, for he felt boys were intimidated by larger schools with too many pupils. His idea was to have the best of the British system combined with Canadian values. From the start it was a dubious premise, as those two ways of life fought each other, but Mr. James pressed on with his idea of thirty-five boys in eight grades. In 1933 Susan Massey donated the family estate, Dentonia, to Crescent and the boys moved to the country. Dentonia had been an experimental farm set up in the 1890s by Walter Massey, Susan's late husband, to provide fresh eggs and milk for Toronto's poor children, who suffered dreadfully from typhoid. It was a cruel irony that Walter Massey died of typhoid contracted from water he drank on a rail car. He was only 37. The Massey family was interesting in many ways, not the least of which their iconic Massey-Harris tractor. The family also spun off Vincent Massey, the first Canadian-born Governor General, and his brother Raymond Massey, the well-known actor. The upper school through whose doors Matron and I had just entered was a fifty-room Edwardian mansion of imposing size to one as small as me, with the first two stories consisting of classrooms and the third set aside for the boarders. The school of now more than 100 students had a ratio of two-thirds day boys and the rest the unloved boarders.

Matron would normally have taken me to meet the head, a Mr. Williams, but under the moist circumstances she felt pity for her charge and escorted me up the formal stairs, normally never used by the boys, to my dorm for the year. Each dorm was named after an English city, mine being Croydon, with London, Newcastle, Manchester and Liverpool making up the rest. Each dorm allowed for six boys except for Croydon which now grew uncomfortably to seven thanks to young Clarke being thrust into it. It was not a popular move, but I was not aware of it yet. Matron left me to my own devices to clean myself up, which I did and then sat on my bed, which had been shoehorned into the corner of the dorm.

These dorms had been servants' quarters in days gone by and had tiny windows and slanting ceilings. There was one large bathroom for the thirty-one boarders, which prompted a sense of lost privacy in me. I yearned for the soft touch of my mother, whom I had perhaps not appreciated enough before. Even the "Austrian" Elizabeth, our maid from home, would have done; I had fond memories of doodling on her large strong arms with the small bullet holes. I was entirely alone. I thought of Sir Walter Raleigh and all those years in the tower before his execution. Miss Payne appeared at the door holding my godfather's letter.

"Are we ready, Clarke?" she asked.

"Yes, m'am," I said sadly. With a surprising quickness Matron sat down on my bed. The scent of lavender sprang from this kind woman, and it is a scent that I associate to this day of a wonderful time in another place, my childhood.

"Please call me Matron, never m'am, all right? Now look here, you mustn't worry, Clarke. Your father went to this school and as I understand it had a marvellous time, so I am sure you will too."

It seemed to me that Father had mentioned being beaten by larger boys while here, but Matron was not to be crossed on a detail. She gathered up my moist clothes and disappeared around the corner, saying; "Dirty laundry goes in the anteroom by the infirmary at the end of the hall, clear?"

"Yes, Matron," I said, as if I had just learned a great secret. She reappeared shortly.

"Come, Clarke, it is time you met the head." Taking me firmly by the hand again, she marched me back down the formal stairs to the headmaster's office below, near the front door where I had first entered this new world.

I then noticed the first truly female property about Matron as she walked in front of me holding the banister, her legs. Really it was her calves I noticed, as the rest of her body seemed to be wrapped in an over-starched type of playing card material in bright white and dark grey. Her shoes were the nurse shoes of the time, with sensible crepe soles and crossed white laces, but from there up to the hem of the body armour formed by the starched skirt a pair of lovely legs appeared, starting with a well-turned ankle that led to a muscular calf. We in the West were only beginning to see the East German women for what they were, the superwomen of their time. Amazons with abilities that seemed to far outstrip our girls. Miss Payne seemed as if she came from the East of East

Germany. Even now my eyes are drawn, well past middle age, to an athletic calf below the cocktail dress.

We arrived at a large and shiny door, whereupon Matron knocked firmly and I cleared my head of Matron's legs. From inside came a cough and then, "Enter (cough, cough), come in," and in we swept.

"Headmaster, may I present our new boarder, Clarke," Matron trumpeted at Mr. Williams, the headmaster of Crescent School, and handed him the letter, which he missed and dropped to the rug.

I stood in a living museum of musty furniture and ancient pictures with a character from the past, a hump-backed frog-like creature in a cloud of smoke and ash trying to stand up and perhaps wondering where his next breath would be coming from. After a gasp or two he seemed to locate it and fell back, exhausted, into his musty chair, disturbing various documents and books. Matron pulled me closer to the huge desk, picking up the letter for another try at the handoff. While not being on speaking terms with Bram Stoker, I could see what the infamous author had meant by "parchment-like skin about the face."

If Mr. Williams was acquainted with the sun, it must have been a brief meeting. His great hooded eyes stared and he wore the disinterested smile of a too full vulture not yet thinking of next week's carrion.

"Welcome, Clarke, I don't want to have to flog you, so see that you don't give me an excuse, like your father did repeatedly (cough, cough), I don't care what people say, I don't like flogging, but it is often, often, the only recourse."

Having finished all that with one breath, he had a terrible coughing fit, one from which I didn't think he would recover. The headmaster then tried to light a Player's Plain cigarette — you remember, with the sailor on the pack. His hands were completely covered by nicotine, and the odour was appalling. Even his mustache, which should have been white like his hair, was an awful yellow and orange. Still trying to light his cigarette while coughing, he grinned at me maniacally so that his stained teeth looked like brown Chiclets looming at me. Matron held me with a firm hand as we waited for the next breath. Suddenly it was over. He took a huge breath, which sounded like wind through Venetian blinds, and said, "Also we don't appreciate cheek around here, Clarke, remember that and there'll be no beatings, not like that father of yours, thank you, Matron," again all in one breath.

Slowly and carefully Matron said, "Thank you, Headmaster. I'm sure Clarke will carry your wise words with him throughout his years here at Crescent, won't you, Clarke?"

I was seven years old and I felt as if I had fallen into the pages of a Robert Louis Stevenson novel. How could I speak, much less speak coherently? I wouldn't have been heard above the coughing so what was the point? I gave Matron a pleading look, but she didn't meet my gaze, she simply tightened her grip on my shoulder.

"Sir," I managed, looking again at Matron, but she seemed to be watching the head carefully. And well she might have, as a great deal more air was leaving Mr. Williams than was coming in.

"Outside, Clarke, and wait for me," she barked.

I did not need to be told twice. I bolted for the door. I didn't know it at the time but I used the last words of the great poet Hart Crane when he jumped to his death from that steamer in the Gulf of Mexico: "Goodbye, everybody!" Stupid but sincere.

I did want to say goodbye and leave these Dickensian creatures to their own devices. How could my father have placed me in such a place after his apparently rotten time at this same school? And what was all this talk about floggings and cheek? I remembered my father talking about the Spartans and their way of fighting. They went into battle naked except for chest armour and shin guards. He claimed they had the ability, learned from early childhood, to shove their manhood up into a body cavity, giving their opponents less of a target. I talked my Grade One friend Russell into letting me try it on him once, which resulted in a few screams that I put down to his inability to relax. However, standing outside Mr. Williams's office, I found some understanding of those Spartan habits, with my Sebastian trying to find a way up into my tummy. From inside the office I could hear, "Breathe, Headmaster, breathe, for the love of God." I could see people running down the hall towards me, for Matron had been heard over the PA system, which had inadvertently been turned on when Mr. Williams staggered into it.

Then the whole school heard, "I am just going to loosen your trousers, Headmaster."

I am like all Clarkes down through the ages, when we don't understand something and are afraid, we begin to laugh. A Clarke did that at the battle of Crecy in 1346, when the Black Prince fell off his horse. Morris Clarke was never heard of again. The same with George Clarke in the War of 1812. When he saw the American troops crossing the Niagara River, he got the giggles and was sent home in disgrace, thus missing the great victory of General Brock over the Americans that day. As concerned staff ran towards the office, they encountered a new boy in the throes of hysterical laughter. When mercifully the PA system was shut off and Mr. Williams had been revived, they turned their attention to me, still softly giggling. A huge master strode towards me, Mr. Noonan, I learned later, and struck me hard on the ear, saying, "Cut along now, boy."

What did that mean? I would have gladly done it, if I knew what it was. What the Crescent School aspired to be in those days was an English public school, although we in North America refer to them as private schools. The difference between Crescent and its overseas counterparts was that it was stuck in a time and place long extinct. Many frightful little boys from the late 19th century would have felt at home at the

Crescent School in the Year of Our Lord 1953. Most of the masters, I came to discover, had been sent down from Oxbridge or the like for the usual — cheating at cards, huge debt or chronic buggery. Many on the staff left for Canada because of all three. One was rumoured to have buried a pregnant lover behind the maid's quarters at his father's estate in Kent, and he had been at the school since 1910. Consequently we were required to speak as if Rupert Brooke were our poetry master. We were forced to pronounce and spell words as they were in the Mother Country ("tyre" for "tire," "kerb" for "curb," and so on). I was disturbed about having to call a "clerk" a "clark," pronounced like my own name. I became, as many boys at those schools were, confused and terrified. I had got out of my godfather's car one boy and entered a world where I had to become someone else, and as they say, there is nothing like a hanging in the morning to focus your mind the night before. I quickly learned the terms those masters used. "Cut along" meant "beat it, kid," "cheek" meant rudeness of any kind, particularly to the masters, and "cloth head," "wet," "joint," "give you a bell" and "to knock one up" all entered my lexicon in a rush for survival.

It wasn't long until I learned a far more sinister term from the boys in the dorm Croydon. To say the least we had a very full dorm with the arrival of yours truly. I didn't have a great number of earthly possessions but even a minimum would tip the balance as far as space was concerned. The situation was not helped by the fact that Matron fussed over her youngest charge, putting a few of my bulkier winter clothes in the wardrobe behind her bed in her quarters near the Great Staircase (not to be used by boys except in the case of fire). While I was getting ready for bed my second night, Jones, who picked at his ears constantly, hence the blood on his pillow, announced, "We are sending that suck Clarke to Coventry, OK, chaps?"

"OK," came a chorus. Then nothing.

"What's Coventry?" I ventured. Not a sound.

"Excuse me, what's Coventry?"

Dead silence. I looked over at Thomas, who had so far not spit on or kicked me, which made me look upon him as dear friend, and directed the question directly to him in a quite loud voice, "Thomas, what is Coventry?"

Nothing again, although I did receive a little spittle from someone to my right. I began to feel very alone and not a little frightened. I fell back on the tried and true Clarke methods.

"Waaaaaaaaaaaaaaaaaaaaaaaa," I wailed and wouldn't stop even after I was assaulted several times by my dorm mates.

I continued: "Waaaaaaaaaaaaaaa, waaaaaaaaaaaaaaaaaaaaaaaaaaa," and Matron appeared at the door in her dressing gown with her hair down holding a flashlight.

"What the devil is the meaning of this? Jones, is this your doing?" she said in a loud whisper. Suddenly the corridor was alive with a sort of metallic coughing. It was Mr. Williams, and he was on a speaker.

"I shall flog the boy or boys responsible for this crushing burden upon my rest at this time at night (cough, cough)," he hacked.

"It's all right, Headmaster, just the new boy, Clarke, having a dream," Matron chirped.

"I will give Clarke a dream he shan't forget for a fortnight, I can tell you, Matron," he said.

It was amazing to me that Mr. Williams had the ability to both hear and talk through his PA system, thus keeping tabs on his school, day and night. I looked over at the other boys. Jones was shooting me daggers from his bed, but in spite of my earlier tears, the sight of the bloody pillow stuck to his ear brought back the Clarke cheerfulness and I giggled. Matron waited for the subtle click of the off switch from the PA system and then shone the flashlight around the room.

"Clarke, come with me," she said. "Suck!" came the taunt from several of the other boys. "Get your dressing gown, put on your slippers and come with me," Matron repeated. "And the next wretch that I hear talking, Jones, I will see that they are gated for a month."

This statement put well and truly paid to all chat for the night. To be "gated," I came to know, was a terrible sentence for a boarder, as one of the few joys of our miserable lives was being allowed to leave school property on weekends for several hours and roam as a pack through the surrounding fields, scaring civilians in the neighbourhoods nearby. Sometimes masters would take us downtown to the flicks, as they were called at "The Crescent School". When gated, a boy could not leave the library for the day. So there were no sounds as I followed Matron out of the dorm.

Matron turned right and started walking down the corridor and I followed quietly with my sleeping companion, Fuzzy the monkey. Fuzzy had brown fur, red eyes and a catchy smile and we had been companions since birth. Matron's dressing gown was shiny gold with a red dragon down the back, not at all what I would have thought she would have worn. By the formal staircase we again turned right and entered the inner sanctum of Miss Payne's life on the boarder's floor.

It was a small, not unattractive apartment with lots of wainscoting and old plaster, almost Elizabethan in its feel. Matron motioned to me to shut the door. We were in her sitting room, which held one overstuffed reading chair of a rich green, and one good-sized couch, which, with a side table, nicely filled the cozy room. Across from the couch was a small fireplace, which held a few fiery pieces of coal, giving a warmth that spread a sense of comfort through me for the first time since I entered the school. Matron poured me a cup of tea with two biscuits and sat down on the couch, tucking her legs underneath her.

"Not a very auspicious beginning, eh, Clarke?" she said as she played with the top of the biscuit tin. "Not what I was looking for from someone of your background."

"What does 'sent to Coventry' mean please, Matron?" I asked, sipping the wonderful tea. This seemed to alarm her.

"Already, Clarke? Good Lord, boy, that was quick. Being sent to Coventry means that you have been ostracized and no one may speak to you. You are a non-person in their eyes. You don't exist."

I blanched, as I was hoping to make the under-ten football (soccer) team and had a feeling that might be difficult if I was a non-anything, much less a non-person. My second full day and I was sent to a spot called Coventry but not really sent, which didn't make any sense, then being told I was a non-person. If I didn't exist why was it that I felt so miserable? And the boys of the school weren't talking to me before I was bloody sent to bloody Coventry, so what did it matter? How I hated the English and their ways. Father said that after ten generations of living in Canada, the Clarkes would never again be cannon fodder for the English. That bold statement seemed to be of no help in my present position, I mean he sent me here. I started to cry. Matron looked at me and sighed.

"Come along, Clarke, you've had a hard time of it, now off to bed," and with that she led me into the bedroom. For the first time the excitement of being in a strange woman's bedroom hit me as it continues to do to this day. Matron returned to her living room to turn off the lights, leaving a small bedside lamp as the only source of illumination. She fussed about in the outer room while I waited with a strange excitement. This was new game that I had never played before, with no knowledge of rules but with an eagerness to please. Matron returned, removed her dressing gown and started to pull back the covers on the bed. She was wearing a sensible long nightgown that covered her from head to toe, but could not hide the bumps of a lovely figure. She was probably around thirty-two at the time, with a face that at best was pleasant when it was relaxed, but out of uniform she was shaped like a fertility goddess. Her chest was ripe, and I could make out the firmness of her thighs as the bed caught her nightie and stretched the cotton across her legs. Miss Payne had been a school captain of field hockey and she was fit. I pressed myself against the far wall, clutching Fuzzy to my thumping chest.

"Get into bed and be quiet, as we need our sleep, and please leave whatever it is that you are holding on the floor — it doesn't look sanitary," she said. I glanced down at Fuzzy. I had never been separated at bedtime from Fuzzy.

"Please, Matron," I began.

"Now there's an end to it, Clarke," said Matron, already in bed.

"Yes, Matron," I surrendered, and put Fuzzy on the small night table from where we could still see each other. I pulled myself up onto the high bed and lay still. It was a fairly large bed, possibly a queen size, in today's parlance, very old with lead paint flaking near the top of the iron poles behind Matron's head. To my horror the springs were also old, creating a large valley in the middle, where Matron now reclined. I clung like a young, recalcitrant bird to the edge of a high nest. Desperately I looped one leg over the side of the mattress to help keep me from rolling to the centre. Matron seemed to be breathing quietly, unaware of my life-or-death predicament. I thought of the inevitability of the situation. I would either cling for as long as humanly possible for a seven-year-old or surrender myself to gravity and get the forthcoming beating over with. I let go.

The night table and Fuzzy passed from view. I came to rest gently against the recumbent woman. There are two sides to every wedge, and I was one of them. The other seemed to be made up of Russell's mother, but I knew it was not. It was Miss Payne, and to be more exact, Miss Payne's bosoms. I wondered what I could use as some sort of reed to breathe through, but then I heard through the massive chest, "Just relax, Robert, try to sleep," in a sort of vibration.

"Yes, Matron," I attempted to say. Now I ask you, could any of you have slept like this? I struggled to get comfortable and attempted to drag myself upwards towards Matron's face. I tried to clutch the covers but they seemed loose to my touch, so I pulled harder, as a little boy would. The "covers" were in fact Matron's nightgown and not just any part of her nightgown but the upper part, so that a vast milky white globe hove into sight.

"Jesus loves me, this I know...." I whispered out of tune, but something else was happening. Matron took my hand and put my quivering palm on the ivory of her bust. Not a word was said. My Sebastian stood up like a periscope on a U-boat trying to spot the coast of Brazil. My stiff companion in life actually made a sound like a balloon being stroked. Matron held my hand against her chest as she started to rub her legs together like some sort of cricket. Not just your run of the mill cricket, but the type of cricket who has spotted another cricket several fields away wearing earmuffs. The sound and heat generated by this odd exercise alarmed me, but it was a warm, delicious frenzy, setting the stage for future entanglements. This went on until suddenly, with shudders everywhere, "Sweet Lord, take me home," Matron bellowed. Just then a metallic buzz came from the speakers in the hallway, but thankfully just an inquisitive buzz and a cough on a search.

"Shhhhh, Matron," I said. "Mr. Williams might hear you."

"Quite right, Robert, now try to get comfortable and sleep," she said demurely. I realized something of great importance had happened but my teeming mind could not grasp what it was. Pondering the problem, I managed to turn my back to Matron and welcome "Nature's sweet nurse", sleep.

I found myself back in the dorm the next morning and life carried on with Matron nodding in my direction only occasionally. I was a little relieved because I just wanted to fit in and draw no undue attention to myself. However I would try now and then to analyze what happened that night. No answers came but I instinctively knew that I must never breathe a word to any of my new friends or it might never happen again. Yes, my new friends. The moment I got back to the dorm I went straight up to Jones and demanded he tell me why I was in Coventry or I would give him a bloody nose. I performed this act of rashness in front of the entire dorm population and Jones gave me a terrible beating for my trouble, but it brought an end to my exile and we all shook hands, although I could have wept in my pain. Matron took me aside later that morning and told me how proud she was of me and I had the first inkling of being appreciated by a mature and knowledgeable woman. It was delightful.

Over the next few weeks I began to enjoy my life at Crescent School. I was in Grade Two in the Lower School, which was situated across the driveway in a smaller version of the Upper School, and I was taught almost exclusively by a Mr. Rudyard Smyth. He was the spitting image of Errol Flynn and yet there was something about him that looked bruised and unsure. He had a slight nervous tick in the left eye, and I romanticized that he had seen things in the war that he brooded on still. The fact was he drank, but he was dear to me and energized my imagination as few other teachers would. Rudyard Smyth taught as if we were in our final year at Crescent. He cared not a whit that the class was made up exclusively of eight-year-olds and one who was just seven.

"Good morning, gentlemen, I trust that you slept well and did not abuse your bodies last night, you dreadful little catamites," he would say. "As our friend Cato the Younger said to Julius Caesar, 'You are wrong, Caesar.'" We didn't have a clue what he was saying, but it was interesting and I became bound and determined to look up the names he mentioned in class to become like our teacher. Plus I didn't want to look stupid in front of the older students.

"Now the way to remember how each of Henry the Eighth's wives fared is thusly," he would say. He turned to the blackboard, pulled back his black cape from his arm and began to write in a beautiful cursive:

DIVORCED
BEHEADED
DIED
DIVORCED
BEHEADED
SURVIVED

And we were off and running into the joys of an education. I could hardly wait to get to Mr. Smyth's class every morning for it was a sweet shop of grand excursions. I do recall Mr. Smyth was continually enjoined by the other masters to stick to the Grade Two syllabus, and not wander through the other grades' territories as this would confuse his students in the years to come. Mr. Smyth would invite special boys up to his room above his class in the Lower School. By special he meant children who were open to expanding their horizons. As doubtful as this sounds he was a gentle man who loved his boys as a teacher. He also helped me understand the school and its inner workings. I had noticed, for instance, that some boys were called 1 or 2 and occasionally 3 and others would be called Major or Minor. It was a code that eluded me. He kindly took me through the steps: "Now suppose you were one of three Clarkes here at Crescent but were unrelated. It would be Clarke 1, 2 and 3 and your number would depend on your age. The youngest would be 3 and the next youngest would be 2 and the eldest would be 1. If you were related and you were the eldest, you would be Clarke Major, the next relative by age would be Clarke Minor and your youngest relative would be Minimus. Clear, Clarke?" He stared at me, his eye gently twitching.

"Yes, sir, I think so."

"Just be happy we have given up the earlier version of Primus and Secundus," and then he laughed a mellow laugh that included us all.

Isn't it true that we always remember the good teachers while the bad ones fade away, with the exception of Mr. Prig, who awaited me in Grade Five? Meanwhile Mr. Smyth would often stop whatever class we were in, and take us for a walk to explain the fauna and flora found on the old Massey farm. He showed us where the snapping turtles hid, where the possum had their cave and which was the best chestnut tree to collect the biggest conkers for our games. He became our hero and we hung on his every word.

Mr. Smyth was able to explain history, not through facts but from the human point of view. He would stroll into class and shout a name, for instance "Napoleon."He would then give us facts and dates but with intriguing foot notes so that remembered. Such as, France seemed almost indifferent to his death on May 5, 1821, after the news reached Paris three weeks later from St. Helena. He told us even some of his old generals were heard making light of it. Yet nine years later there were as many as fourteen plays and exhibitions about the emperor playing in Paris at once, all of them favourable to Napoleon. He related to us the last words of Madam Du Barry, the royal mistress to Louis XV, to her executioner in 1793, "You are going to hurt me, aren't you?"

Mr. Smyth got into hot water finally after reading Genesis to the class, the part about creation. When he got to the phrase about God resting on the seventh day, he turned to the class and said, "Does it make sense that the world was built in six days while yesterday we discussed fossils that are approximately 20 million years old. Hands, please, yes, Coyne." He pointed at a High Anglican minister's son who was waving his hand. Mr. Smyth loved to stir the pot, sadly.

"Yes, sir, it does, because it is not how long God took to build, it's how long it lasted, that's the point, sir," Coyne said. Mr. Smyth loved the parry and thrust with young minds.

"Very good point, Coyne, but now let us ask, how old does the Bible say the Earth is?" he asked. The trap snapped shut on Master Coyne.

"Six thousand years, sir," said Coyne.

"Correct. Now how do we account for the slight difference in years between a fossil at 20 million years, and the bible world at 6,000 years, not to mention the six-day build, Coyne?"

Coyne turned a deep gray mould colour and slumped down in his desk. The class cheered as Coyne was a stick in the mud and preached an early version of the "God will get you" sermon at us daily. However it was never a good thing to mock the teachings of the Bible at a Church of England school. The next day our class was visited by a beet-red minister and a more pale than usual headmaster.

The Reverend Coyne and Mr. Williams sat at the back of the class, paying close attention to our teacher, who suicidally started a discussion on the book of Revelations. He reminded the class that Thomas Jefferson had called it "merely the ravings of a maniac." This brought God's servant to his feet. "Mr. Headmaster, I am not about to sit here and let this man talk about the living word of our Lord in this fashion," the Reverend bellowed as his son smirked at our master. But Mr. Smyth was made of firmer stuff.

"Sir, are we to take literally the idea of the Four Horsemen of the Apocalypse or the Great Whore of Babylon?" he asked.

"I say, Smyth (cough, cough), steady on. There are children here," the headmaster interrupted.

"Or the Number of the Beast, 666?" continued Mr. Smyth.

"This is outrageous!" the Reverend cried.

"I will (cough) see (cough) you in (cough) my office straight away, Smyth," screamed the headmaster. Shortly thereafter a prefect from the Upper School arrived to fill in for Mr. Smyth. I am not sure what happened in that office but he never brought up the Bible again. He was allowed to finish the year but did not return the following one. We never saw him again. Thirty years later I discovered that he had returned to his native England, leaving no address or phone number. The next time I was in the U.K., I did a little detective work. I found a distant cousin of Mr Smyth's who explained that our hero from all those years ago had been clinically depressed since childhood and was unable to hold down any employment, especially after his stint in Canada. A few years after his return to England he had slipped into a canal in the Welsh countryside and brought an end to his short life. Rudyard Smyth was thirty-one on the day of his suicide, a great teacher who went unrecognized and unrewarded. His story will haunt me always.

CHAPTER 5

(The return of Mrs. A and Grace. Some of the more licentious elements have been removed and yet it retains Mr. Clarke's original spirit. Ed)

Now might be an appropriate time to return to Grace and her mother Mrs. A and to what started that afternoon at the May Fair. I had pretended to have visited the Shetland Islands off the northern coast of Scotland. What a bloody awful place Scotland is and was. There were more Scots on the English side at Culloden than on Prince Charlie's. They even handed over their great hero Wallace to Edward 1, Longshanks, to have him publicly disemboweled. Only Scotsmen could have founded a place such as Winnipeg. Did one of them stop in the dead of winter and say, "Och, here's a graaaaate place to live, no you think?" Are you kidding? Still to Grace they were wonderful and that was enough for me.

I read everything I could on the place just to please her, for I had grown quite fond of her in the weeks since our "accidental" meeting. I could rhyme off the Firths as Forth, Tay and Moray, likewise, the largest freshwater lake was Loch Lomond and the deepest, Morar. And it was working, for my groping had taken on a more sensuous quality new to Grace. She imagined soirees like those of the Bloomsbury hothouse flowers before the Great War, where free thinking and free love were rampant. I hurried nothing as she burbled about this poet or that one and their untimely deaths. Actually the death part did worry me a bit, as there was far too much talk of it for my liking. She came up with the bizarre idea of slicing our ankles and just before expiring, we would make love one last tragic time. I pointed out that as we had yet to make love, perhaps we could put off the death scene. She left the subject alone yet I knew that the thought lingered.

Her father struck me as a decent enough chap but a little slow on the uptake. He was an actuary with a large downtown insurance company and as dry as a stick. He had a personality given to understanding facts and figures and took great joy in announcing that most men will die at seventy-four. This left a lot to be desired for dinner conversation, but I was happy to fill the gap. Mrs. A seemed to hang on every word I said. In fact she remains the best audience I can remember having. Her big green eyes raked over me while she smiled a lazy smile. Mr. A looked a bit at sea while he struggled with the usual underdone meat on the menu at the A household. Grace prattled on about Vita Sackville this and the Mitfords that. All in all, things were building to an interesting but explosive end.

Grace phoned one afternoon to say that her parents would not be home till the following day. I took on the air of supernatural indifference as I was still a little put out about the previous night. In spite of the fact I had come up with a perfectly good apartment and a not bad bottle of wine , Grace had once again declined my invitation to lose her virginity. I did I know have a bit of a rep for chasing virgins at that time, far too much trouble now I am afraid and so tiresome but that was then as they say. It was just I could have slotted a sure thing like Susan Collins who was definitely not virtuous, but ever so happy to oblige., thus saving me from the dreaded "blue balls"

I can remember telling Linda somebody it was a medical condition that could cost you your life and that there were special wards in some hospitals exclusively for men beset by it. Linda, a student nurse, said she had never heard of the malady and perhaps would ask her roommates about it when she got home that night. How could a student nurse in 1966 think there could be something called "blue balls"? The old saying held "If you can't get a date, get a nurse." I think she was from out west somewhere. Anyway Linda then tried to call the nurse on duty, a friend, and ask her. In desperation, I proposed marriage to try to keep her from using the phone as I could see the evening going up in flames.

She clearly had some experience in the lovemaking area, but I am not sure what I did about the impending marriage at the end of the evening. I can still see her with her freckles and small nose, but I don't remember her body, strange that, as I usually do with the body and not the face.

I have been with many nurses in my time and they fall into two categories, Very Knowledgeable, or No Knowledge. It is either their first day holding a Sebastian or they grab it roughly like an old mate that has been avoiding them, and some of them don't believe it when you say that you don't want a colonic, thank you. I have staggered out of more nurses' residences than Heinz has pickles, badly bruised and focused entirely on finding the nearest bathroom.

Anyway, here was Grace calling, ready to make amends with the happy coincidence of her parents being away. So Grace's loss of innocence took place that evening in her parents' bed after an undercooked lamb shank with mushy peas. She suggested we go upstairs almost immediately after the meal, for which I was thankful, as I had caught an eyeful of her so-called apple crumble, which looked like she had failed desserts as well as main courses.

Mr. and Mrs. A's bedroom looked like the Vatican on a big speech night. There were large candles and small candles, round candles and flat ones, candles from trips the family had taken — there was even one that looked like a cat. You know when you turn on the news at eleven and they show a fire chief shaking his head and saying, "Kids smoking" or "Faulty electric." I suddenly had a picture of the fire chief saying: "Must have been a coven. Two bodies burned beyond recognition and a thousand candle sticks."

If that wasn't enough, the family had a cat, which happily ran through the maze of smoking candles. I like cats, Biscuit for instance, but no cat I know would have been caught dead in this place, not with this heat. I felt a trickle of sweat run down my back. With one eye on the cat I watched the beautiful Grace slowly take off her clothes. It became harder to see her through my red rimmed eyes. Grace disappeared, I think into the other room, returning, covered in scarves. Now if I had wanted Issy Duncan, I would have asked for her. Grace carried on, unaware that I was not at all impressed. Boys, I should tell you, are only there for the main event. I admit that I had pulled out my old friend to stroke in anticipation and to make sure Sebastian did not fall asleep in the heat and boredom. She then put on some awful music, which sounded decidedly oriental but certainly not catchy — more like a dirge for a not very well liked dowager of some sort. Then Grace spotted Sebastian.

"Put him away. I am not finished yet," she whispered. Put him away? Still I did as she asked. So I watched her dance with scarves and things around the room, while I sat there like a bored Herod, wondering if she would bring me the head of the crazed cat, which ran between her oscillating feet. Finally, the record ended and she flopped onto the bed beside me, looking for approval. I applauded dutifully, then got about the business at hand.

Unfortunately Grace's exertions amongst the candles had caused her to perspire greatly, putting one in mind of a busy gym. This was a case of "Be careful what you wish for," but in my defense, I did NOT wish for a dancing dervish with music from a small, obscure province in China, I did NOT ask for eleven hundred candles blazing away around me and I most assuredly did NOT ask for Tuffy the Cat, who looked like Peter the Hermit scuttling about.

What can a chap do? There was Grace absolutely naked beside me, breathing hard. She still looked lovely but she appeared more like a patient about to undergo some sort of medical procedure wondering why the surgeon was wasting time. No doubt that generations of male Clarkes were wondering the same thing as they looked on. It seemed as if Sebastian had gone to bed with cup of cocoa and a good book. I was alone.

Grace shut her eyes as the yearly Virgin Sacrifice must have shut hers in her canoe, going over Niagara Falls. This was all in a split second because in another split second Sebastian was up and about, the cocoa forgotten. I remembered Major Iggulton's rifle instruction for the slope arms maneuver: one two three- one two three- one! My Sebastian went from a small pistol to a Bofors gun and I was away and running. I must say this, and I am proud of it all these years later- Grace fainted. It was all too much for her. It gave me a bit of a bad turn. It however was just for a minute or so and then she was back with us. I can still see her after the event, propped up on one arm babbling about how she now knew what the poets were talking about.

I left out one thing. Early in the proceedings, Tuffy the Cat had got it into his tiny brain that I wanted to play with him. The first I knew of it was when he dragged his claw slowly down the length of my right leg. Most chaps would have said, "Right, that's it, I'm off," but not a Clarke. I ignored him and continued my efforts with Grace. I waited until he came further down my limb so I could flick it off with my other leg. But I flicked a little too hard. There was a sort of squeak, followed by the sound of rushing air as something moved across the room, and then a thud.

Cats have not made it through a hundred million years for nothing and landing on a Tiffany perfume spritzer combined with a shell comb up the backside did not faze Tuffy. After a brief pause to gather his senses, he returned to the bed in a less playful mood. This time he stayed high on my thighs. My leg shot about, but the cat was no longer within the circumference of my kick. The good news was that Grace enjoyed the new rhythm and laughed as I continued my blind search for Tuffy.

There are many ways to torture a man, but I have always been drawn to the Visconti family, which resided in 13th-century Milan, and in particular Bernabo Visconti, the lord of Milan. He was the father of an event called the Quaresimo, which consisted of forty consecutive days of torture administered to some poor soul. The idea was to do a little something each day on behalf of the state, perhaps a broken leg here or a plucked eye there, all in the main square of Milan. At the conclusion of the forty days, what was left of the poor victim would be disemboweled thus ending the entertainment. My point is that if Bernabo had been aware of Tuffy, he and his brother Galeaszzo might have considered adoption: Tuffy Visconti.

Finally the cat struck and sharp little claws sank into my scrotum. The pain would have brought applause from even the Circuses of Caligula. I rammed into dear, innocent Grace, knocking her hard against the ornate headboard, and carried on up the large window curtain with the cat still attached. There is a whole school of thought that would say Tuffy was the victim, as I had startled him and therefore he clung on for his life, but I'm not having any of that. He knew exactly what he was doing; only weak-minded liberals would save him from the scaffold. I pulled desperately at him with tears in my eyes, but he clung even more tenaciously. The room began to turn red before my eyes, and finally the curtain gave way, sending the screaming cat and me to the floor. The cat legged it, and I was left to explain myself to Grace. Luckily she seemed to think it was all part of the experience, so I left Tuffy out of my explanation and went in search of soothing balm for my shrieking bag.

I know this isn't telling the story about Mrs. A, but I am coming to that. First, however, a universal truth, in my experience, at least: once girls get a taste for it with what they now assume is their "True Love", they want it all the time. Through the following weeks Grace wanted to "have a go" in terribly uncomfortable forums: parks, telephone booths, cars, even a cloakroom at the club, where we were discovered by an outraged Major-General looking for his great coat after lunch. I was even assaulted not once but thrice in a graveyard, and as I was on the bottom for the performance I became a kind of human brass rubbing. Disgraceful and I could have caught my death of cold.

I had started to avoid Grace, as it was all too much, plus I was now in pain from over-exertion. Strange isn't it really.

I came back to Toronto, determined that I had had enough. I arrived fairly late at Grace's family home, and Grace told me everyone was out. As every chap knows, you may have the firmest of resolves when it comes to saying goodbye to a lovely girl, but when faced with "one for the road," it takes a man of Herculean staunchness to turn away.

So once again I walked up those well-trod stairs, thinking that after more over-exertion I would give her the bad news. Since I had kicked Tuffy into some leaves outside by the porch, I began to relax. Grace seemed a little different. There were fewer candles and scarves, more of a determination to get to the main event. As I began to get down to the business I heard an odd noise, but I put it down to Tuffy flinging himself at a window so I paid no heed. A split second later I felt something wet on my leg, like a tongue, but that was not possible as I was staring into Grace's eyes. The cat must be back, I thought, but how? I cast a wary eye southwards and took in the sight of a semi-nude Mrs. A kissing my leg.

I pause here for a little background on my relationship with Mrs. A. For months I had been delivering Grace home after our dates. When I brought Grace into the living room , I know we both emanated the telltale scent of earthly delights. Mr. A would wiggle his nose and say something like "Had fun, did we?" sticking his face back into his paper, while Mrs. A would offer us tea before I took my leave. However on the nights when Grace's father had gone up to bed, Grace would often be sent off to the kitchen to prepare a late-night snack, leaving Mrs. A and me alone. Inevitably Mrs. A would be in a loose-fitting dressing gown with a tendency to open, asking me pointed questions about our love life: "Call me Carolyn, won't you? Surely Grace is not enough for a boy of your experience," etc., etc.

I always enjoyed those times with her. The excitement level was great and her interest in everything I did seemed genuine. Before her daughter would return with the tea and biscuits Mrs. A. would rest her hand on my knee for an extended length of time until Grace sat down. Grace would occasionally say, "Please, Mummy, do leave Robert alone." I put it down to her being a lonely old woman. She must have been all of 45 years old. Funny now, of course.

As I stared at the Mrs. A. Grace suddenly became aware that we were not alone. It was now obvious to me why Grace had been in such a hurry. Mr. A had dropped Mrs. A off first before taking their other friends home in his car. I was well and truly stuck for words, as I am sure all of you would be. What was the etiquette in the present circumstances?

I fell back on the tried and true: "How are you tonight, Mrs. A?" Then my boilers shut down and I became a mute. What was I to make of an acquaintance of my mother's with no bra on? And her breasts did not look tired at all — they were magnificent. Grace began to berate her mother.

"How dare you enter my room like this, Mother?" she shouted. "I just want to be a facilitator of your love for

Robert," Mrs. A said. That threw me a bit but before I could say anything, she began to form the three of us into tableaux that had only been seen, I was sure, in the rougher edges of third-century Rome. It was as if Mrs. A was passing the torch to her daughter, but first wanted to prove that she was the acknowledged champion, and I must say she had a point. Grace didn't object outside of the occasional sob,

"How can you, Mother?" and "My God," for she and I learned a few things that night.

When I am a very old man (as I am not there yet) stuck in a rocking chair on a veranda somewhere, I will be one of the lucky ones, filled with great memories and few regrets. In short Mrs. A did a shocking thing but I look back on it fondly and would not change it for anything. Mrs. A would be about 90 now and is probably ignored, as most seniors are, but the stories she could tell! I hope she is well. Grace left for Europe shortly thereafter to finishing school in Switzerland, and I am not sure what became of her. Mr. A took early retirement a few years after the incident with Grace and her mother and died on a tennis court in Florida. It was a very Canadian death. Mrs. A was well provided for.

CHAPTER 6

(Clarke's first flogging at Crescent but sadly not his last. However these descriptions give a living testimonial to an almost forgotten chapter of the post-war period. Ed.   )

I must return to my days at the Crescent School, for it was there that much of what the world now sees as Robert Clarke, Esq. (Clubman) was formed. First of all our dress. Every day we wore the same thing to school: a grey Harris tweed jacket with a white shirt and either the school tie or our house tie. There were three houses at school — Hudson, Wolfe and Mackenzie — and every student belonged to one of them. I was in Hudson. If you were over five feet tall, you could wear grey flannels for trousers, but if you were under five feet, like most of the Lower School, you wore breeks in the winter and shorts and high socks in the summer.

The breeks, sometimes called breeches, looked like riding pants or the kind motorcycle cops wear, even a variation on the famous jodhpurs, wide around the hips and thighs but close-fitting at the knees. These were also made of grey Harris tweed. One did up the laces from the knees down to the mid-calf, then pulled grey socks up over the laces to keep things ship-shape. We were forced to wear an indescribable little cap, which rounded out the impression we were English war orphans. There was also a formal school blazer in the school colour, a dark forest green, with an outsized silver school crest on the breast pocket. Students wore that ensemble on special occasions such as prize day; otherwise we wore a matching grey Harris tweed jacket. Matron said I was her little soldier, at which I burst into tears and won another night in her bed.

I am not sure whether you have ever felt unlined Harris tweed, but I am almost sure Nero used it on surly Christians in place of their usual hair shirts. I have such sensitive skin that I can't abide even mildly scratchy material. I am told that when I was a baby, my mother loved to dress me in bonnets of all kinds and colours, which I didn't mind as long as they were cotton. I was happier than most babies to be chucked under the chin by the big-bosomed Austrian nannies on my neighbourhood pram rides. However put a bonnet on me that was wool or some cousin of wool and big-bosomed or not, they were for it. I became completely enraged. I bit any chucking finger that came my way. Mother, at her wits' end from my bawling, stuck me out in the garden, whereupon I would spend hours struggling to remove the heinous hats. Often they would find me with the hat completely covering my face, with the back of my head and neck taking on an alarming puce colour. So when I stuck a tentative leg into my first pair of breeks, in seconds I decided I was not having any of this foolishness and to Matron's embarrassment, I refused to be fitted at Eaton's College Street Prep Shop, "the Home of Canada's Schools."

Poor Matron, who had been given a clothing allowance by the school on behalf of my traveling parents, standing in the boys' section of the Prep Shop with Mr. Tyler the tailor as I screamed at the top of my lungs.

"No other boy has lined breeks, Miss Payne, I can assure you of that, and I know because I do them all," Mr. Tyler said. I didn't like him much and besides he spent too much time checking the inside of my pant leg. He would whisper things like, "You have been naughty, haven't you, boy?" and things like that.

I soon came to the realization that one screaming child would not change the school, so I put on the terrible breeks, in pain the whole time. Matron as always promised me a way out. On the way home to the school, she said she would try to line them herself.

Dear Matron, where are you now? Do you ever think of the time we spent together? I hope so, for I will always remember you.

The point of all this was that one looked like a little boy until one became five feet. I would look at the taller boys as they glided about the school in their long trousers as if cast in a stage play about the sophisticates of London. The rest of us were either socks down and dirty knees or in those wretched breeks, and me waddling in an effort to keep the barbed wire of the Harris tweed from attacking my young testes.

In an effort to reach five feet, we hung by our legs from trees, we sat on each other as still others pulled our legs, and we ate huge meals, which made the dietitian complain that the Lower School might have a case of virulent worms. Some amongst us shot ahead of the rest and waved goodbye to us shorties and then sat smugly near the seniors as if they were our betters. Bah and double bah!

Some boys developed faster than others. We could not help but notice in the showers that Padullo, a black-haired Italian kid of stocky build, had a substantial amount of pubic hair, while we had not a hair between us. I began to look earnestly for any sign of down between my legs and would often sit in class with my hand down my front fingering the area, ready to welcome any forlorn curly hair that might appear. To my everlasting shame in Grade 3 Mr. Hughes caught me with my hand stuck in my breeks. Shouting, "Perversion is everywhere and must be stamped out!" he dragged me to the front of the class with my hand still cemented to my front, wanting to know whether I was part of some touring fakirs presenting long-forgotten stances or was I, as he suspected, playing with myself, in spite of the knowledge that I would become blind in the fullness of time. I died a thousand deaths, but I kept up the inspection, just a little more secretly. As for perversion Mr. Hughes left the school in disgrace years later for the crime of having a foot fetish. He was caught in the junior boys' locker room smelling running shoes.

Crescent was in many ways an idyllic place for a young boy to form in those early years, and by form I mean to take on substance. There we were on a huge property, allowed to roam at will, and to live in a castle-like building with food and drink served every few hours or so. In the junior dorms, my friends and I formed gangs and acted out crucial points of history, egged on by the one or two less senior masters on duty through the weekends. Mr. Gillies would suggest the Spanish Inquisition, with me wanting to play the sinister Torquemada. My friend Leverty always wanted to be the Dominican friar Hernando Martinez, who butchered 6,000 Jews in Spain for not being Christian, even when it was pointed out that Martinez's deed was done a hundred years prior to Torquemada.

We all wanted to be villains, and we had teachers who were young and truly loved teaching, no matter how they came to be there. Only Mr. Prig and Mr. Williams frightened us. They were the real villains in our lives. The masters were an eclectic lot. There was Mr. Noonan our PT (for "physical training") teacher from the Australian navy, who was thought to have thrown someone overboard for being "rubbish." Whether it was true or not, one quailed at being called "rubbish " by him. He was the most in-shape chap I had ever seen up until then, with a chest that seemed to go straight out from his lower neck and then back to a stomach made up of rivets. He would insist that we play soccer in the most inclement weather, wearing nothing but loose-fitting shorts, a singlet with only a scarf as a nod to the freezing temperature. He was mad, of course, but terribly amusing in the way he saw life. It went by in clear stages: "Bloody born, you bloody get in shape and then you bloody well die." And then howl with laughter at the whole thing.

If you asked him too many questions about his life, it was "Bloody kids, let's go for a bloody run," and then it would be five miles cross-country led by a man who never seemed to get tired. His motto he said he got from his doctor father: "Hurt bloody no one."

For a man who loved to fight it must have been meant more as a silent philosophy than actual deeds, for fight he did. Often on Mondays Mr. Noonan would appear for our first-period PT looking like he had done his forty days of the Quaresimo, with his face bruised and beaten from what he would only describe as "a bloody lucky header," which we took to mean a head-butt of some kind. The school turned a blind eye to his punch-ups; we always wanted to see the other guys. He also had a wife who we rarely saw and a brood of children, which never appeared. When queried he would only say, "You lot are my bloody children when I'm here." We would say no more in fear of another cross-country run. To this day I use the word bloody far too much, thanks to that man.

Then there was that dreadful man, Mr. Prig in the fifth form, which for some reason was called the Shell. Again no explanation, just the Shell, and of course, "Shut up, Clarke, cut along now before I thrash you," which I did with great alacrity. I had taken the strap a few times before I got to the Shell, the first way back in Grade 3, through no fault of mine, a cry perhaps I have overused through my life, but in this case it's true. There I was minding my own business in English literature, taught by Mr. Aird, a most talented teacher in all ways but one.

He had a pronounced stutter, which only became worse under stress just like that chap at Whitney, only no singing. He had been moved to the Lower School to accommodate his affliction in the so-called friendlier lower forms. On the average day he would foist the usual Shakespeare upon us in the last class before lunch. The Bard has always been a take it or leave it subject for me, but I still went in later years to Avon and Stratford, in other words, I did my bit for his nibs whenever I could and it was expected anyway.

There were, unfortunately, a few things Mr. Aird could not abide, one being the theory that Francis Bacon or the Earl of Oxford were the real authors of the so-called works of Shakespeare. It was Ben Jonson who pointed out "his small Latin and less Greek" culled from the free grammar school nearby made it seem highly improbable that William Shakespeare could become the Bard. Still there it was, an argument for the centuries. Mr. Aird wasn't having it and that was that.

I had a great friend in Grade 3, Meloche was his name. I also had the maddest crush on his sister Patience. She was older than us by a few years, which I discovered meant a lot when I pledged my love to her upon our second meeting. She looked at me as if I was something unpleasant on the bottom of her shoe, saying; "Go away, you disgusting little boy." I wanted to point out to her that Henry the Second was fully fourteen years younger than his wife Eleanor of Aquitaine and yet they had eight children together. Still she shunned me: "Ugh, go away, brat."

In the 1,500 years that the Clarkes have strode the earth not one had I am sure been called a brat. I gathered up my torn dignity and removed myself from her presence, a wiser lad. Perhaps it was fitting after all that Henry had locked Eleanor up for some sixteen years late in their marriage. I now understood what had been a closed book to me before. Still Meloche remained a good friend, as he had warned me against the charms of his sister.

Meloche had a sadistic streak and he loved to goad Mr. Aird at every opportunity. The lesson began: "Booooys , wwwwwe willll open our texts to RRRRooomeo and Juliett, by WWWWW" at which point Meloche shouted "Bacon!"

"W W W W W W W W W W W W W W W W W W W W W W W-
Wiiiiiillllllllllllllllllll…" Mr. Aird tried.

"Francis Fried Bacon," my seatmate interrupted.

Mr. Aird began to take on a dangerous colour and fairly shouted, "Shaks Shaks Shaks Saks SHAKS SHAKS FUCK ME SHAKESPEARE!!!!!! " He shook his finger at Meloche and tried to say his name: "Meeeeeeeeeee …Meeeeeelllll.." but gave up.

Unfortunately he could say my name and pointing at me, he said in clear tones: "Clarke, pressssssssent yourself to the headmaster to be punnnnnnished for gross cheek."

Can you imagine the unfairness of this? He couldn't get Meloche's name out, but he could mine, therefore I was guilty. If my name had been Abramowitz, I would still be looking forward to my next trip to the Tuck Shop and acquiring a Turkish Delight chocolate bar, my favourite.

Mr. Aird seemed unrepentant, as he had been forced to curse while stuttering in front of his boys and now someone would pay. Down through history there are many examples of the innocent paying the price for the guilty because of expediency. One of the clearest was of unimaginable evil, one Cesare Borgia. A town called Romagna was defeated by Borgia but remained a dangerous place, so Borgia appointed a psychopath named Remiro d'Oreo to restore order. He did this in remarkably short time through brutality and slaughter. Then Borgia had d'Oreo beheaded in the main square as if to say, "I am shocked this had been going on, I had no idea and let me say how sorry I am." It brought a smile to Machiavelli's face when he later wrote about it.

However I was on my way for my first of many strapping. I was also forced to carry my sentence in the form of a scribbled raving from Mr. Aird. I walked slowly from the warm surroundings of the Lower School to the cold grayness of the Upper School I felt as the English soldiers of Edward the Second must have felt when marching towards Sir James

Douglas's castle in the marshes between England and Scotland, knowing that Sir James had butchered every English soldier that had entered before. He also had a bad habit of taking his time with captured English archers, removing certain fingers and taking the right eye before the formal torture.

I dragged my trembling nine-year-old legs towards the large front doors, with the boys in the second-floor grades looking down with interest, much as the citizens of Rome looked down upon the Christians soon to be croissants for the peckish lions. I handed Mr. Aird's missive to Mr. Williams's secretary, who looked at me with dead brown eyes before disappearing into the headmaster's office. To my right on the way in was a Turner print of some Lake District scene and I wondered whether it would be the last beautiful thing my blue eyes would see before my execution in a few minutes' time. I made a pact with myself to visit the spot should I be lucky enough to survive the coming ordeal.

The thought of being strapped was so horrific at that age one could barely imagine life after the event. I had been hit with a ruler at Whitney, even the backhand cuff of a teacher's hand, but had not received this sort of formal punishment. The masters would grin and mutter about corporal punishment being a forgotten black art, that they were going to petition the headmaster to show some leadership in this area. This was NOT a school based on the idea of "spare the rod, spoil the child."

There was Mr. Senior, who had a wicked throwing arm with either chalk or the chalk-brush. He could pick off a lazy child while barely looking at his target from the blackboard. Many a boy appeared at lunch with a bruise to the forehead or a thick ear from Mr. Senior's 11:10 a.m. French class. In spite of that we loved Mr. Senior. He had been captured by the Japanese in Singapore. The war had started before he had finished medical college in England, so he had volunteered as a male nurse to the Far East and witnessed horrible crimes the day the Japanese captured their front line hospital. He never recovered from seeing his patients bayoneted in their beds and the female nurses, some in their seventies, raped and mutilated. He only survived because when he objected to this abominable treatment, he was stabbed and left for dead but somehow lived. When the second wave of troops came through he was classified as slave labour and sent to work in Burma on the so-called Burma Railway, including the bridge on the River Kwai, and then in Japan in the mines. At the end of the war he weighed 76 pounds.

He had no time for the nay-sayers against the nuclear bomb dropped on the orders of Mr. Truman. "We could see the distant flash and we loved every moment of it. We were saved and I didn't care if every Japanese citizen perished after what they did to my friends and colleagues," he said. He would also go mad about those who felt pity for Japanese-Canadians who were interred during the war.

"It was war and the Japs were shelling the west coast of Canada, plus they had landed in Alaska. Don't forget, boys, the bombing of Pearl Harbor was a result of American-born or assimilated Japanese spies letting mainland Japan know what was going on. You should have seen what they did to Europeans caught in Japan the day war was declared."

He never forgave the Japanese, and his stories of torture, executions and willful neglect haunted our dreams in the dorm.

As I stood looking at the Turner picture and thinking of how afraid Mr. Senior must have been during the war, I heard a cough in the sanctum, indicating Mr. Williams was ready to deal with me. I no longer cared about Mr. Senior, as his woes could not have been as bad as this. Sure he saw beheadings and bamboo shoots stuffed up the odd arse but not a strapping.

"(Cough, cough) come (cough, cough) in, boy."

I entered as Edward the Second must have entered his last cell, tentatively and with great alarm. Sure he was one of the worst kings England ever had to endure, but did he deserve the final act in 1327, planned by his wife and her lover Mortimer at Berkley Castle? Even today on September 21, I say a small prayer on his behalf, for his fate was horrible. His executioners had orders from his wife Isabella to leave no mark upon him, so with a torturer's creativity, they shoved a white hot poker up his fundament.

As I entered I couldn't help looking for a radiating brazier and smoking poker or two. Mr. Williams stood by his desk, eyeing me as a mongoose eyes a miscreant snake. He lit a cigarette with relish and was about to say something, no doubt unkind, when his body shook with a cough. Then another, and another, and one so huge that it dislodged his cigarette from his brown fingers, whereupon it fell onto the patched Persian rug. He struggled to the windows, which he threw open to get a breath. His back was to me as he hacked away and spat into his handkerchief. It took all of ten minutes of coughing and sputum for Mr. Williams to rejoin the land of the living. Whilst still looking down at the courtyard and a few frightened scullery maids, he gasped, "God (cough, cough), I hate children." After a few more coughs and a final spit into his wretched hankie, he turned to once more take in the image of a frightened little boy who had done nothing wrong.

"It is my unpleasant duty to beat you, Clarke, yes?" What was I supposed to answer to that, but like all monsters it was rhetorical. "Unanswerable down through the ages." I pleaded with him that it was another, not me who should be here, and like all my ancestors I was prepared to name names.

"Stop sniveling, boy, for I had the same unpleasant duty with your father in this very room and as I chased him about the room, which I trust I won't have to do with you, I reminded him then as I do you, boy, that if there is some small injustice about this thrashing, then it's only because you had gotten away with some earlier outrage and it all evens out in the end."

What was I to do? Well I wasn't going quietly, that's for sure. As I began to look for exits to make my escape Mr. Williams sprang forward with alarming dexterity and held me by my forearm. As he pulled me towards his desk, I could see what was in the open drawer: the school strap. The newly invigorated headmaster held me like the blind man had held Jim in the Admiral Benbow Inn at the beginning of Treasure Island, cruelly, with vise-like strength, all the while covering me with his appalling breath. He started to cough but held me close as we rocked with each spasm; I feel the buttons of his waistcoat on my face to this day.

The cough stopped and the moment had arrived. He whipped from the drawer the instrument of death and held my hand out.

"Open your hand, boy," he whispered and coughed his bear-like breath. I kept my right hand clenched in a ball. He now began to breath hollowly and with difficulty,

"I shan't tell you again, Clarke," he said. Please let him die, Lord, I prayed fervently.

I opened my hand and the first stroke of any strap ever hit my hand. I opened my eyes. Mr. Williams was looking at me less like a mongoose and more like an interested professor wondering how the specimen under glass was faring.

I was still alive. He hit me again. It was not the end of the world and this would pass. Turner could whistle before I would visit that stupid wooded glade. It was a lesson learned early; as Caesar said, "A coward dies a thousand deaths, but a brave man only one." I took three strokes on each hand, which hurt but not to the extent advertised. I had survived my first strapping, although I still blush when I look back at my cowardice under fire. Still I was the school hero for a few wonderful days as the youngest to be formally beaten and with the added bonus of Matron taking me to her bed for well-deserved succor.

I became more and more acclimatized to the rigors of private school. I made true and trusted companions amongst the boarders while I learned the ersatz ways of the English remittance-man masters. Whatever the weather, we played sports. Soccer continued into December with Mr. Noonan out there in his scarf, shorts and singlet yelling, "Up, boys, up!" as he ran us through endless matches. The old leather ball, which was pre-war, as was all our sports equipment, became so leaden with moisture it's a wonder we didn't break our toes, as it was like kicking a large garden ornament.

This madness, however, got us in fine shape and we developed far beyond the average grade school child: two hours of sport five days a week consisting of one hour of PT and the other of organized sport. Now as I order a large gin and tonic, I give thanks to those sports masters who are responsible for my still fetching figure at this late stage in my life. Which reminds me, I don't think I mentioned the pool. The Masseys had built a wonderful indoor pool looking out into the courtyard, heated, mind, and entirely constructed of terra-cotta tile. Even as stupid little boys, we recognized the beauty of the place. We loved swimming there and it was a central part of the after-hours country-club atmosphere for us boarders. However my first day was not one that I will dwell on too long.

In these type of schools all boys were expected to swim whatever their ability. Furthermore you had to be naked. I knew about the first part, sadly not the second. I was so looking forward to that first plunge, as it had been one of Uncle Tony's sales pitches that I had managed to hear through my crying: "WWAAAAAAAAAA — and how —AAAAAAAAAA — big is the pool —AAAAAAAAAA?" I managed to get out.

As it was, it wasn't very big, possibly 35 feet by 15 feet for 100 boys, but to us it was Olympic. I could swim like the proverbial fish from all those summers at the family cottage, when mother would worry about me spending too much time in a wet bathing suit. She would shout from the cottage screen door, "Robert, you will get a rash you know where if you don't get changed."

It was the third day of school in the autumn of 1953 that the call came to those in the Lower School to make our way in an orderly manner to the pool. We formed into twos as Mr. Smyth indicated, trooped out onto the lawn, then turned left and followed the paving stones to the Upper School, then down into the courtyard and the entrance to the pool.

We had all been assigned a locker, which now contained the flotsam of our first soccer games plus our gym kit. As we approached our lockers, I couldn't help but think that my bathing suit was actually upstairs in my dorm and when would I be told to "cut along, boy" and retrieve it. It hit me that I was the only one with a worried look on my face.

The lockers were along a thin corridor outside the pool area. The floor consisted of large, rough red square tiles, the same tiles the Masseys had used in their stables. It was still early September and yet the corridor could have doubled as an autopsy storage room. When I think of that floor today, my feet curl with cramps from the well-remembered cold.

Everyone began to throw off their clothes in preparation for the promised swim, but not a lot was going on. At that moment the pool doors swung open and eighty upper school boys came out of the pool. Eighty wet, nude boys. There was chaos as they tried to pass, shoving us into our own lockers with the haughty disdain older boys had for their lessers. That didn't bother me. It was the other part.

"Mr. Smyth, may I go to my room and….." I started to say.

"We all go as we were born, boy, that is our way, as the Greeks taught us," he said, cutting me off. I had never been naked with my contemporaries before. Clutching my privates I followed the others through the pool doors.

CHAPTER 7

(Clarke has a fling and gets his picture taken for free......
shocking.....We have taken the liberty of concealing her correct
name. In the end of course we don't even know if it's true as there
has been no exhibition that we have been able to find in spite of
Mr. Clarke's demise. Ed)

I would be the last person on earth to eschew nudity —
all for it, always have been. From this table where I am sitting
with my large gin and T, I can look out over to what used to be
the library and smoking room and is now the women's dining
room, and know that at one time or another most of these
women, drunk or sober, had visited my pied à terre. I recall
one Christmas party I took advantage of three of the bejeweled
herd, two in the women's sauna and one in the squash court,
without the proper shoes. You will notice that I used the term
"took advantage" as a sop to the ladies involved, should it ever
come out. All three cut me dead when they saw me at various
times over the following weeks, no secret smile or raised
eyebrow of recall, just the steely expression of feux virtue.

There was a time when I would draw admiring glances
from the fairer sex, when eyes would sparkle with unspoken
promises and "what might have beens" passed silently between
innumerable girls and me. No more. My son refers to me as a
"sad little sack of history;" I am not at all sure what it means,
except it doesn't sound very attractive. It is true that women,

even when I am wearing my best London suit, pass by me as if I was begging in the street. "Off the subject, Clarke,as my fifth form Latin master used to say.

As I stared over at the women's dining room, the second table on the right seemed to be spending an inordinate time looking in my direction. One of the group seemed to confer with her nest-mates, then staggered to her feet and tottered over towards me. After a few "tots" she rested, clinging to a startled waiter serving a retired Supreme Court Judge, and after a small contretemps continued atop her uncertain legs towards me. As she hove into view I realized who she was and our mutual history shimmered up in front of me.

It is a sad fact that my regard for women is not at all returned. They seem to place me in a box containing mountebanks, lawyers guilty of sharp practice and diddlers of small boys. With all the so-called Pride Parades cluttering up the streets, one would think women would appreciate the dwindling chaps that are left, such as I. Not a bit of it. I would have been frog-marched from this club eons ago but for our family history at the B&R. The Badminton and Racquet Club sits on land behind the old Fran's restaurant, which was at one time the public gallows, where one could view the uplifting event of some deserving fellow getting his neck stretched. When the more sensitive elements of society suggested the popular activity be moved indoors because of inclement weather, the lands were purchased by the founders of the present club, namely my family. So as much as they try to see the last of me, I fully intend to roost right where I now sit until my innings are over.

There was a time when there was a "turn-away business" in the matter of being my betrothed, and I was known as a bit of a "Jack the lad". What happened? I will tell you what happened: I hold the secrets of a generation and they are scared as hell. But instead of being kind and friendly, they avoid me like the plague, only calling upon me at events when all and sundry are tipsy. Well, my pretty ones, won't the ears of your future offspring be burning when they get an eyeful of this memoir.

"Good God, Sally, we'll have to resign from our club," some gobsmacked husband will say.

"What on earth are you talking about, Rupert?" will answer the innocent relative of one of these present day Lizzie Bordens.

"Ahem, 'Sally Spencer seemed to have an inordinate interest in Sabastian as she licked and kissed him for well over an hour in the headmistress's antechamber during the annual tea dance at Havergal School,' it reads in Chapter Two," says the anguished husband.

"Not my great-great aunt Sally!" (Weeping.)

"And … and it would appear that a good portion of Chapter Three is dedicated to your mother's very thorough rim jobs, as they are referred to, and her continuing predilection to anal sex!"

How happy I will be, gleefully rubbing my hands together in my warm grave.

Back to the moment. As the woman made her way unsteadily past me, she managed to lean down and say, "What are you writing about us, you imp of Satan?" which just goes to show you what happens when a chap with my rep does a little jotting in his Birks notepad.

I smiled and wished her well. I recalled after she stumbled away that she was the older sister of one of my conquests, which she clearly had not come to grips with. Happily sitting at the table behind hers were two attractive young women. It is possible in this life, in spite of one's years, to become aroused on certain occasions and completely caught unawares. They sneak towards you when you have turned away for but a second or two, and as you return, the sap rises again.

Of the two, the one closest to the club's marble fireplace impressed me the most. She too flickered her eyes towards me, yet she kept her attention riveted on her companion, maintaining an equilibrium that appealed to this old rake

Presently her friend took her leave, whereupon she picked up the financial section of that morning's paper and dove in. I finished my first brandy of the day, put my linen napkin by my finished plate of tasty Welsh rarebit, and with my heart pounding like a pursued fawn, was about to push myself up and make my way towards her table.

I have been grateful for many things in my life, even those acquired purely by happenstance, such as my sterling eyesight. I have stunned many of my male friends by the sureness of my baby blues, pointing out, for instance, sports bras from distances know only in the animal kingdom, thus helping a friend avoid any possible forced exercise after a hoped-for tryst. A chap wants nothing more, in the post-coital world, than a comfortable bed and a conversation turned in his direction, not a potentially life-ending jog.

It was this acute vision that picked up a slight movement from my target, so I managed to camouflage my attempt to gain my feet as adjusting my trousers after a well-deserved lunch. I sank back into my William Morris chair and waited. The lovely creature folded her paper, shot me a laser-like look, stood smartly and strode towards me. My heart began to leap, and I wondered if I had snagged the errant nose-hair seen this morning in the rude magnifying mirror. How I wished I had used the facilities to check for the inevitable food stuck between teeth, not to mention the possibility of impure breath heavy with brandy. Too late, but damn it, I am an old man and cannot be expected to be a show horse at this stage of my life.

I gazed at the Ionic balustrade near the staircase as if deep in thought, which of course I was, although a little more shallow than my look would appear. She stopped at my table and looked down as I looked preoccupied with my already read paper.

"I am sorry to bother you, but do you mind if I speak to you for a few moments?" she asked. I had coiled my legs and with a firm grip on the table, I shot up and stood through most of her inquiry, giving the impression of a much younger man. It is a trick taught to me by a great-uncle who would have made love to a pile of bricks. He is purported to have had a romp with his female Chinese acupuncturist just before he expired following a good lunch at the ripe age of ninety-five.

"Please join me," I said. "May I order you a little something?"

"A Remy, please," she responded as Sebastian suddenly lurched within my trousers. I deduced that she must be an affiliate member from a sister club in some other city as I had not set eyes on her before and yet she had signed for her meal with a flourish.

I was correct. She was from some club in New York City with the word "women" in the name. Her name was Natalie and it turns out she was, and still is, a famous photographer, her work appearing in those appalling fashion magazines. Let me tell you what she was staring at. I am as hair-free as a cue ball, thanks to my mother's side of the family, and slightly jowly, this time as a result of the Clarkes and their weak chins. Other than that Natalie was looking at a sixty-something man in a $2,000 suit with all engines racing.

We made small talk about the failure of clubs to maintain their covenant of superior righteousness towards outsiders. Perhaps those were my thoughts, but she seemed terribly interested and encouraging. I was about to ask her opinion on flogging when I was forced to reverse arms in the face of the waiter arriving with our drinks. Natalie swirled hers in a crystal glass, part of the set sent to the club by Raglan of Crimean War infamy. It was said he looted them from Nolan's tent, perfectly understandable under the circumstances. Raglan's gift was in honour of Major Dunn, Canada's first Victoria Cross winner, won during the Charge of the Light Brigade at Balaclava in

1854 and a past member of the club. I prattled on about these and other subjects while Natalie sat in what seemed a state of wonderment.

I wish my own children had paid more attention to me when they were younger. It would have done them a world of good, as is clear from their present situation. I can't blame their mother for everything, but I can blame her for laxness on a lamentable scale.

Natalie smiled a Cheshire cat smile throughout, rarely letting her gaze fall from my eyes. We were locked as it were, and it was a pleasant way to take one's alcohol. Finally, when I took a breath, she said, "Would you mind sitting for me?"

I wouldn't have minded having an afternoon romp perhaps in the cloakroom now that the lunch rush was over. As it turned out, she wanted to take my photograph. Still, not bad, I thought, a chap my age and a famous female photo artist wanted to take my pic. March on.

"Of course, my dear, when would be a good time?"

"If you are not busy, we could get on it right now," she said. Sebastian stirred in his bivouac.

She had the use of a studio owned by an artist who was recovering from attempted suicide over his badly reviewed opening. What could I say but yes? Just when you think life holds no more surprises, along comes a Natalie and the long-ago spring returns to an old man. We made our way to the artist's abode and within a few minutes new drinks were poured and I waited anxiously for my chance to be a muse.

I was taken back when Natalie threw the giant overhead lights on, as it put me in mind of sad Ruthy. So far this was not turning out to be the tête-à-tête that seemed so certain at the club twenty minutes earlier. Oh well, no fool like an old fool, so I sat looking out the vast window at the rainy day that it had become in drab Toronto. Natalie approached with the look of a worried mother on her face. "You are not very happy, are you, Robert?" she asked.

There was no point in beating around the bush. This was not working out to my satisfaction. Natalie sighed and then took a breath.

"I had been looking at you through lunch for a reason, Robert," she said. "I have never quite seen a face such as yours before."

"Eh?" I said wittily. "What was that?"

"When I look at you I see a lion in winter, a Tiberius living out his life in Capri, and it is something I want to capture," she said.

A lion in bloody winter? I thought that was Henry the Second with all his family hating his guts. My family did find me tiresome, perhaps, but not a bloody Henry. As for Tiberius, every child knew that Tiberius lived in splendid Bacchanalia on Capri, yes, but only till that little creep Caligula grew tired of waiting for him to die and put a pillow over his face so he could be the new Caesar.

I did know I didn't look my best in this type of lighting and perhaps should be making a start for home when Natalie dropped the bomb. "My idea is to photograph you as I see you and all the history of your being…….."

"Which means……?" I said apprehensively.

"I take you in the nude."

I looked deep into her eyes for irony. There was none. There came a great rushing sound in my ears and Sebastian stirred in his cramped cubicle as she added, "And as you know it is the unspoken mission of the artist to make her subject comfortable, in order for the art to come to the fore."

What now?

"Please use that room at the end of the room to disrobe. There is a bathrobe for your convenience," she said.

"I will act as your lion in winter, my dear, but you must disrobe as well," I responded.

"Anything for my great Caesar." She smiled a dazzling smile. I darted for the little room at the end of the studio and was fairly panting as I closed its door. I tore at my Jermyn Street 200 pound-sterling robin's egg blue shirt, all the while wondering whether I would be man enough for her at this late date in life's calendar. "Please, dear Lord, let me have one last time at spontaneous love. Please stop my friend Sebastian from doing you know what prematurely or going like a baguette forgotten in the rain. Just this once, Lord, and I will go back to St. Paul's Bloor Street. I know what I said last time to the rector after his sermon in favour of same-sex marriage: 'Is it not a strange world we live in, Rector, where sodomy is good and smoking is bad? Good day to you, sir!'"

The riposte had pleased me no end at the time, but perhaps looking back I was a bit brusque. I know what you are saying, "Why isn't our hero carrying a little pharmaceutical helper?"

First of all if one has had the broad life that I have, one should be able to conjure up a huge reservoir of erotic images from the memory banks to more than compensate and two, a friend had a heart attack.

I walked back to the harsh lighting, which had been subdued in the interim. A white couch stood bathed in soft yellow light as Chet Baker played in the background. Natalie stepped forward dressed in what we used to call a "boiler-room suit," a one-piece affair of light tan with a zipper up the front. She looked every inch the attractive artist while I'm sure I looked ridiculous in a black bathrobe with red stripes running amok on it. No wonder the owner tried to jump off a building.

I stood there while Natalie fussed with the massive camera. I could not get over the fact that I was not in charge. This would surely end badly, and I had so wanted to impress this beautiful American girl.

"Now, perhaps you could remove that hideous cloth coat and present your wondrous body for immortality," she said.

If ever words could galvanize a man my age these were they. I stepped royally out of the robe and stretched out on the couch. The lights and the sudden draught momentarily stunned Sebastian, but together we waited for whatever this marvellous girl had in mind. She readjusted the camera to the very much live subject, for just then Sebastian crawled lazily across my stomach. Natalie tried not to look but smiled at the sight nonetheless.

"Robert, your friend is ruining the perspective," she said.

"If anything, my dear Natalie, it would be ruining the proportion," I lobbed back. She gave me a devastating smile as a reward. There is nothing like impressing a Bryn Mahr girl. It must have been somewhat like Margaret Bourke-White smiling down at a mud-splattered Marine in WW2 before snapping his photograph.

With my pump racing like a rabbit I watched as Natalie fingered the zipper at the top of her one-piece. I could have stopped and discussed that great Canadian invention, the zipper, but now seemed not the time for nationalism.

I have always enjoyed people who don't rub one's face in it when they honour a deal such as Natalie's and mine. It shows style and breeding. This was the case now as Natalie came towards me as if on a slow conveyor belt, pulling down her zipper whilst keeping her eyes engaged with mine.

"My lovely old Visigoth, exhausted from the sack of Rome…."

"First accomplished in 410 AD by Alaric the Visigoth, while so many think it was Attila, who was first in 452 although technically he was bought off by Pope Leo," I whispered helpfully.

"You must now enjoy the fruits of a lifetime of labour, Alaric, by taking any woman you wish." Her suit hit the ground.

"You," I croaked, pointing towards her. What followed was series of mouths, tongues and body parts, which would no doubt have pleased old Alaric for it certainly did me. What a great time for an elder statesman such as myself. These kinds of trysts were well behind me, or so I thought.

After a suitable time I opened my eyes, as a gentleman always allows time to pass in these situations. Natalie was arranging a full-length mirror on its side so that I could observe myself, with not a word about our shared recent event. She walked towards me with two large glasses of what turned out be a fine Chablis, very cold and very dry.

"Robert, you are aware that I am drawn to your face with its chronicle of victory and loss, and you are also aware that I very much wish to photograph your face and your body, leaving nothing out," she said seriously. "I am doing this all over the world. Wherever I go, I search for my lions and you are my new find."

I sipped the wine nonchalantly. She pushed the large mirror on its casters into the pool of light near where this lion in winter lounged. I raised a heavy eyelid and looked into the mirror.

"Great scalded cats!" I exclaimed. In the mirror was what can only be described as something subhuman found, after many rough months, in a not very nice landfill. I stared in disbelief. "You can't take a picture of that, they will have you for abuse," I shouted. "This is Elder Pornography."

She started to laugh a whiskey and cigarette laugh. If this was intended to disarm me she was mistaken. I was well on my way to getting a full head of steam up. Alaric would have known what to do and no waiting. He would simply have given her to his troops for their amusement, and that would wipe the smile from this "user of old men."

"Oh, Robert, you are wonderful," she said. "One can see what you must have been like as a young man. Don't worry, the lighting will help, as will the black and white film."

She showed me some Polaroids she had snapped when I first arrived. I looked quite distinguished in a few. Some of the fire left me. "What about the nude part?" I tried.

"Darling, I need all of you, as I think I have proved," she explained. "Now I want to get you into immortality where a man of your gravitas should be."

It all seemed very reasonable but for what looked back at me from that mirror. That wreck was not what I could have imagined as me. From the curled toes up the blotchy legs, the thighs that once were steel now hung from their moorings. The stomach sagged sadly over my shriveled testes and there was no sign of the oft-bragging Sebastian, tucked up out of sight somewhere. The rib cage looked like a xylophone in need of repair, and the chest seemed to be sitting on itself several times over. My face, which appeared so pleasant and strong above a bespoke suit and a tightly knotted club tie, now seemed like a three-day-old red balloon with the air slowly escaping. And over this entire train wreck was the obligatory sprinkling of liver spots, which I had always more or less considered large freckles.

I wanted to weep, so I sat up and put my feet on the ground and my head into my hands and buried my face. FLASH went her camera. I looked up, full of outrage that my moment of introspection should be assaulted in this fashion. FLASH-FLASH-FLASH, again and again went the damned cameras, and I stood up and waved my finger at her.

"Is even this is to be denied me?" I reproached her, which she immediately wrote down.

"You, dear man, have the most wonderful lexicon I have ever heard," she chirped. "You are stuck in the wrong age, Robert, you are a Renaissance man if there ever was one."

" But look here," I whinnied. "I can't have photographs like this circulating in public."

"Surely you are aware that men at your stage in life are attractive to many of us because of the very way you look," she said. "Every one of your lines and imperfections tells a story of a life lived long and strong." I tried to cover myself with a purple throw. "You are worried that there will be social repercussions from the exhibition of these glorious portraits of you, yes?"

I nodded dumbly.

"I do not exhibit still living persons, Robert. These photographs will only see the light of day after you are dead."

I now saw how Margaret Bourke-White had handled the Mahatma Gandhi, who until he met Margaret had only wanted to play with his granddaughters.

After a little sobbing I sat for the portraits and by the look of those Polaroids, I began to take on the majesty predicted by my American beauty. She not only shot me sans clothes but with that purple throw that I had earlier used to dry my eyes. I looked like Shakespeare's Caesar, I am glad to say, rather than Mary Shelley's Frankenstein, whose spectre had given me such a fright at the start. Shelley wrote her classic in 1831 on the shore of Lake Geneva, whilst staying at a hotel with Percy, her husband, and Lord Byron. Because of the rainy weather, Byron suggested they all have a go at writing ghost stories while waiting for the sun. Mary wrote the story of Victor Frankenstein and his monster while the others gave up and went back to their sugary poetry.

Before I left, Natalie insisted that on behalf of the continuing good relations between our respective countries we should have one more round and for a man of my experience to be taught one or two more things about the black arts of the bed sheets was a gift from that riotous young woman.

Walking along that blot on the landscape called King Street East, I couldn't help thinking that somewhere sometime, a marvelous exhibition of my ruins, well earned and wise ruins, mind, will be talked about and admired, and what sweet revenge that is. While most of my contemporaries sat at home clipping coupons and watching the telly, I was cavorting with a thirty-two-year-old thoroughbred full of intelligence and Thai love secrets, so that my testes were empty and my memory full.

CHAPTER 8

(The pool incident. I have once again endeavored to ascertain the truth, but much seems to have passed into legend as all of the main players are either incapacitated or deceased. Therefore make of it what you will; I pass no judgment on its veracity. Ed)

Back to Crescent School. It had just hit me that I was going to have my first nude swim. To be sure, we had gone skinny dipping at summer camp, but that was in a lake at night when you could not see your hand in front of your face. I even hated that because I wandered into what must have been the Ontario version of the Sargasso Sea, where I was almost overwhelmed by the lake weed. In fact, but for the scream coming from the boy next to me when I had grabbed his balls in silent terror, which alerted the authorities, I might not be here. Now a new terror faced me as I shot through the pool doors almost frozen from running on the cold floor to face twenty boys throwing themselves happily into the waters of the heated pool. Nude or not, the water felt great and soon it was if clothes had become an offense to me and I might never wear them again.

I was about to dive from what I hoped was the deep end, when I caught a movement outside the windows. They were fogged from the condensation of the pool but I could just make out two faces. I signaled to two of my friends and the three of us snuck along the side of the pool to just below the window. We paused, and then jumped up at the window with a yell. The dietitian and Mr. Williams's secretary stopped gawking at us and left their feet in fright, while we shot into the pool, denying any involvement.

In the weeks ahead we waited for those same observers each swim day. The first week there was no sign of them but by the second week they were back, with cigarettes held high as their excuse to be outside (although from the amount of smoke inside the school one was never forced outdoors). There they stood, two of the most hated people at the school: the dietitian with her black hairy arms and the secretary who showed not an ounce of kindness to the victims standing outside the head's door waiting for the strap. It was said she grinned at the sound of each smack. They were there to look at young boys' naked bodies, that was clear.

So we hoisted Batten up onto the radiator under the window and pushed his bum hard so that his genitals spread across the front of the window. We held him there until he started screaming from the heat of the radiator, then let him back into pool, cursing and holding his feet. The women loved it. We couldn't hear what they were saying through the window but by their smiles it seemed to be the highlight of their day. We became more outrageous as the weeks progressed, with each one of us trying to improve on the other's affront. Since I was the only one uncircumcised, I would roll my foreskin back and forth, to the great interest of the dietitian. She would put her nose right to the glass and focus on nothing else. If my heel had not started to smoke, we might still be there.

The end came quickly and with a shock. A few weeks later, Morgan gave the wave from the window, the signal the women were back, and we once again gathered under the window thinking of something more spectacular than the last encounter. What was odd about all this was in the course of our daily routine, when we saw one or both of the women, there was never any recognition that anything had happened.

This time we thought of something that might stop them in their tracks. We had heard from some of the Upper School boys about a game called buggery. If it was to be believed, you took your Sebastian and attempted to insert it into your male friend's tulip. Batten and Jones Minimus were to be the players in our pretend story; Morgan and I were the lifters, all of us naked as on the day of our birth. When our targets started their walk towards the window, we counted to three and hoisted our two friends up onto the radiator. We looked to see where Mr. Smyth was; he was reading from his book of poetry at the far end of the room. Jones Minimus bent over with a stupid smile on his face as Batten started smacking his bum with his body, back and forth, back and forth. A great rhythm was going.

I paused in my struggle to keep them upright to look at the reaction from our regular observers and found myself looking into the face of a perplexed Mr. Williams in the company of two open-mouthed prospective parents and their understandably gawping and horrified child.

Being a Clarke through and through, I bolted for the safety of the pool, leaving Morgan to do the heavy lifting. Mr. Williams began to pound the window with his fist. Morgan let go of everything. Signals had already reached the players above that not all was well, first the shakiness below, then the strangeness of the greeting from the audience outside, which sounded like cats fighting over fish, followed by the complete structural collapse of their stage.

In a flash Morgan was in the pool, trying to hug me out of fear, and the other two were in free-fall. Jones Minimus landed first, on his head, bouncing into the pool, while Batten alit awkwardly on the radiator, sliding down its steamy side. Jones Minimus came up jabbering about spectres at the window and Batten began waving his arms at the same moment the headmaster rounded the corner of the pool, going at a good pace for someone in the fourth stages of emphysema. With a cry of "They have left the school and shall be suing!" he shot across the tiles in his leather shoes and into the pool, scattering the stunned children.

It became clear that on Batten's slide down the radiator, his genitalia had become lodged between the pipes that ran in parallel lines down the side. These, as Batten indicated in castrato-like shouts, were exceedingly warm, and if it wasn't too much trouble could someone come to his assistance quickly?

Meanwhile we almost drowned poor Mr. Williams in his heavy black robes as we all jumped in to assist him in order that he might remember us well in case of future floggings. Batten had begun to wail. Mr. Smyth was trying to organize the head's rescue and really hadn't noticed Batten much outside of a mental note to chasten him for staring out the window rather than helping the rest.

I put it down to Matron that Batten is now a grandfather, although the offspring may be a little undersized as a result of this mishap. Just as he was slipping into semi-consciousness, Matron rounded the school pool, followed by Gord, the school handyman. She grabbed a bucket and started to pour water on the inflamed area. While Matron poured, Gord took an enormous spanner, attached it to the end knob of the radiator and began to turn it in an effort to cool it down. Boiling water began to spurt from the knob, landing on Batten, who was off for another run.

"Stop it, you fool, you're cooking him," shouted Matron, who began to apply some sort of grease to try and ease his swelling and very colourful manhood. Suddenly some boy shouted, "It's Matron!" It was as if twenty naked boys had just bitten into the serpent's apple and had a sudden collective thought: "We are naked and Matron is amongst us!" Once more Mr. Williams, who had been making his way to the side of the pool, almost lost his life as a slew of boys churned the water trying to make their retreat. As he went under again, Mr. Smyth leapt in and pulled him to safety.

We boys had all reached our lockers in the deep freeze of the corridor and quickly changed into our uniforms, for once happy to be back in those warm Harris tweeds, and then tore outside to the pool windows to observe our friend Batten. There he was at the middle window, his fogged face grimacing through the leaded pane. Every so often you could see Matron's face pop up to look at how her patient was doing and then return to her task below, as Gord stood stupidly by with the spanner at the ready. Using a strange wrist action and a year's supply of balm, Matron finally released Batten, who, with a look of melancholy and fatigue, swooned at the feet of the handyman and Matron. Poor Batten had scarlet loins for the rest of his life and is known even today as Bacon Batten.

Life went on at Crescent as advertised, and I became more and more a product of that school. In the autumn the boys tried to find the largest chestnut for the game of conkers. This age-old English pastime was accomplished by driving a nail through the centre of a chestnut and then stringing a shoelace purloined from someone else's plimsole through the hole, knotting it and then aging the weapon for a week or two.

In the game, one of the two players offered up his conker to be hit by the other contestant. If the conker survived the blow, then the reverse took place and so on till one conker was destroyed. This took hours of our time as we passed about recipes for hardening our weapons with polish and Dubbin. It seems so long ago and perhaps silly but I loved the games and often wish for a piece of string with the friendly weight of that hardened chestnut back in my trouser pocket.

Between conkers, soccer, gym, swimming and the first whiff of some game called cricket plus enormous amounts of homework, the order from Mr. Williams's microphone for lights out came as a tremendous relief at 9:30 each night. We awoke via a bell, which sent us tearing to the bathroom for tear-inducing relief from the previous night's hot cocoa. There were only so many toilets, four I think, so many of us took advantage of the handy sinks, which I preferred, as one could also brush one's teeth as well as examine one's face for a hoped for whisker.

CHAPTER 9

(The very unfortunate incident in the men's washroom at the B&R Club gives us some insight into Robert's closed-mindedness and lack of understanding of the very multicultural country we live in. Most unfortunate. Ed)

This brings up a painful episode at the club during the Christmas do. Have you noticed the world is now awash in politically correct hogwash that seems to have replaced a thinking man's logic? Take, for instance, this idea that every culture that arrives on our shores is to be celebrated as some sort of iconoclastic revelation. That's all well and good, but here in this club I have seen changes that threaten the very underpinnings of the institution. Those of us who choose to make use of a very good cigar while at our club, one my family has been associated with for 150 years, must now do so outside of its salutary confines. We are thrown out the door as if we were leftover filleted fish. Typically after lunch we troop out the side door to stand by the portal under which reside the dumpsters containing all the club's outrages. My friends and I stand there like back alley abortionists, rain or shine, and attempt to somehow enjoy our $75 Cubans with a modicum of joy. This is outrageous, especially when the smokers' section offered to fund a room with exhausts strong enough to draw that poncey new manager of ours into their blades. Not a bit of it, so here we stand, ostracized to the great outdoors.

They have also hired female waiters, who must be spoken to nicely and cannot be kicked. Why the other night I was forced to explain what a Manhattan was. The final indignity is female attendants in the washrooms! Our founders are spinning in their graves as I write this; in fact, I hear a moaning sound from the late Brigadier-General Piggott-Jones.

"Say it is not so, my boy." he says plaintively from his restless sleep, as do the rest.

The female attendants would cut close to the bone for old Piggott-Jones, as he was caught rogering his batman in one of the stalls by an elderly attendant with the General claiming he was so pie-eyed he thought it was his niece (once removed). So much of that sort of thing was quietly painted over in those days.

I had always given the Men's amiss when I saw the little signs reading, "Warning, female attendants are cleaning, please use caution, The Management." So I suppose the inevitable was bound to happen. One evening I was dining alone as usual when I spotted an elderly lady who had got separated from the rest of the herd. Her friends had taken an interested party on a tour of the women's section, with this one choosing to sit out with her large glass of brandy. She must have been all of seventy but one could detect that in her day she surely had been a beauty. As we eyed each other, each thinking of the other as an after dinner mint, I could feel a substantial piece of overdone roast beef caught in a bicuspid. I nodded at her and indicated that I would return shortly, then made my way towards the men's toilets downstairs. I had virtually grown up in the club so that I knew everything there was to know about it. I knew, for instance, that at this time of night, the toilets by the dining rooms would be used by the braver of the male staff and so would not be as fresh as I liked, but the downstairs ones would still be up to my sanitary standards. I shot down the grand stairs as a young boy would, caught up in the throes of the chase and seduction. In the white-tiled bathroom, I took the handy nail knife I had stolen from Richart, that dirty German, 45 years ago at the junior cotillion, and began to softly prod for the food. As I was thus employed I realized that a good manly pee might be called for before I returned to the Siren. I had consumed one gin and tonic, a bottle of Pinot Noir, followed by two large brandies, so I damn well deserved it. I was standing at the friendly sink and doing quite well on the meat-in-the-teeth front, but I was gasping to make water, a problem for Solomon if there ever was one. "Bugger it, it's a men's club," I thought, and in a flash I was peeing in the welcoming sink and working on my teeth all at the same time.

The point was I was happy at my club, which is after all the point of having a club at all. Suddenly, a woman appeared right behind me. It turned out that she was a cleaner and that I had inadvertently missed her presence advertised in a very small sign at the entrance of the men's toilet.

I said pleasantly, "Ahhhhhhhhhhhh."

The bloody woman started to scream. If there is anything that sends shudders down the backside of club management it is a female screaming in the men's toilet. I admit, as came out at the board of inquiry (more like a kangaroo court if you ask me) that I should not have subsequently sprayed Mrs. Mammereet Nabir by turning in her direction thus causing her to subsequently burn her entire wardrobe, and forcing her and her outraged husband to go on an unexpected Hajj to bloody Mecca. But what chap wouldn't have been startled into turning in the direction of the commotion, particularly if it proved to be a woman coming from the previously thought empty stalls of the men's room? I pointed out at the club inquiry, that my doctor had warned me against any interruption whilst using the urinal,

"No interruption of flow," is how I believe he put it. Terribly upsetting for the waterworks in a man of my advanced years.

Anyway with the yelling and whatnot there was all hell to pay for my little trip to bathroom. Needless to say there would be no tryst with the woman waiting upstairs or with anyone else for that matter. In minutes my lovely club had taken on the uglier aspects of a Salem witch-hunt.

I was aggressively asked by management to not frequent the club while evidence was being gathered. Evidence! I admit looking back that I should not have used the club sinks for anything else but their usual function. Guilty, and let's move on. Not a bit of it, because the woman involved would not let the bone go.

In the past you would you simply take all the change out of one's pocket and thrust it at the bloody woman and everybody goes about their business. My present children take an inordinate delight in chortling at my naiveté for assuming that people are still IN SERVICE, which is why I don't see a good deal of them now that they are of majority, the ungrateful sods.

In days long past many chose service as a dignified profession, one to be savoured. People actually looked forward to running and getting things for fifty years, then to be pensioned off to a room above the garage. What a wonderful life to look back upon as the carbon monoxide lulled you to sleep each night in your cantonment. But now we have women in men's facilities.

I spent two weeks at a much lesser club hiding, for all the good it did me, because clubmen talk amongst themselves so that for not the first time in my varied life I was to be avoided. You would think I had been part of bestial sex ring the way I was treated. Several former friends cut me dead upon meeting me in the library of the Royal Military Club down on University Avenue.

"Nice day," I said brightly, meeting two of them carrying large drinks to the reading room.

"Mmmmmm," replied one, not meeting my eyes.

"I am afraid I don't know that one, Binky. Perhaps you could sing a few bars," I said as they swept past me without smiling.

" Oh, I remember, it's called RUN BINKY RUN," I said loudly at the retreating backs of Binky Butler and little Wilson Minor as I knew him in the fifth form, Upper School, Ridley, who tore into a slumbering footman while making their escape.

Bah! What has this life become, banished from my favourite club, plus the silent treatment from two chaps at a downmarket club? I was not sure I could carry on. Should I move up to my cottage in Muskoka and talk rubbish everyday at the local Tim Horton's? No, a thousand times no, for I am a city boy through and through and a clubman to boot, I am not interested in local lunch specials, although their tea is quite good.

At the appointed hour, I walked into the George the Fifth dining room to the right of the main dining room. It was the closest to a Drumhead Trial outside of the military there could have been. The club swine had placed a long table in the middle of the room, which had five chairs along one side. Off to the right there was a small table with two chairs, matched by another setup off to the left, clearly for the use of guilty and the prosecution. In a nice touch, all three tables were covered with green linen from the card room. That bloody-minded aggrieved woman and someone who looked not unlike the Vizier Sinan the Assassin occupied the table to the left, while mine faced the sun through the large windows behind the committee table. I had asked our family lawyer to perhaps stick his head in on the gathering, but… "You did what!!!!!!!" he said when I explained the situation calmly and fairly.

Once his regular breathing returned, he begged off — something about a week of prepaid tango lessons. Abandoned! He worked on behalf of our family for almost 35 years, during which time we never, never questioned a bill from his firm, and there have been some damn juicy ones. Now like the rest he runs as the proverbial jackrabbit runs when most needed. Bah! The man ought to be horsewhipped.

All this for peeing in the sink. This is not my fault. There weren't enough toilets for thirty boys first thing in the morning at school. Why is it that in any other trial they could bring in a cultural expert if it was a native or other culture and talk about how I was brought up, miserably in a dorm without my parents. But no, as we types are left to fend for ourselves for we have no discernible culture I feel like I'm living in the last moments of Rhodesia and how are we loving that chap Robert Mugabe these days eh?

Anyway, the Nawab sitting with the Houndess of Hell was a chap called Faizul Aqqab Siddiqi. It was explained to me very slowly by the club committee chairman that Mr. Siddiqi was the chairman of Islamic Studies at Guelph University and was here at the request of the Nabir family.

"Isn't that a veterinarian college?" I said. At the time it seemed to me a point of interest for all in sundry but it brought the first of many chills to the proceedings.

" O Crusader, do you think I sit with pigs? " said a beet-red Siddiqi, " O tremble in the Prophet's glare, O bad man! " All the while he shook his finger at me. I got the Clarke giggles, which made the committee extremely uncomfortable and the little man with the funny hat tear at his hair. The long and the short of it all was that I was made to write a groveling apology to the really marvelous Mammcreet Nabir and pay for their bloody Hajj, (I hoped they would get trampled) plus give an enormous amount to the Staff Christmas Fund. There was worse to come.

"Mr. Clarke, the committee, after much discussion on this point would put it to you, that Dear Mr. Siddiqi has come up with as he says," A Path To Forgiveness," droned the chairman. I had sat there for nigh on four hours listening to bilge about Infidels and Crusaders without any offers of refreshment other than tepid water. There is nothing like a lecture in broken English, on 7th and 8th century history to sharpen the taste buds, not to mention the kitchen smells of the hugely anticipated lunch, only to have all hope dashed in deference to the man with the funny hat, hummus would be served.

I'll give you history! The Prophet felt ill after his return from Mt. Arafat (wasn't that the name of that bloody Palestinian terrorist) and just couldn't make it to see his nine wives, but did have a favourite, Ayeshah whom he had married at the ripe age of NINE, so he dragged himself over there and promptly died in 632 AD. If he wanted more history there is always the story of Mohammed 2nd, the Ottoman sultan who took Constantinople in 1453 by using the first real cannon. When the walls fell, such a slaughter of the inhabitants followed that it took several days for the sultan to get control of his marauding troops. He finally put a stop to the carnage by loosing his warrior monks onto his own troops, with the result that more soldiers died at the hands of their own people than in the actual battle for the city. The monks also sacked the most beautiful church in Christendom, which strangely enough has never been returned to the faith unlike the Mosques in Jerusalem after the 67' war.

I was about to tell this story in rebuttal when something in the eyes of Mr. Siddiqi suggested I stop, something a Clarke knows when to do, excepting Bernard Clarke, who had inside knowledge of the gunpowder plot against James the First in 1605.

He thought he heard the Parliament buildings blow up and started singing,

"The King is dead, oh, the King is dead and I did it, I am a Catholic, ha ha," in front of a group of stunned patrons of the Licking Duck Public House. Unfortunately, the explosion was attributable to an unwise baker. Outside of that headless

Clarke, we pretty much know when the audience is getting restless.

As the lunch smells wafted over us, the chairman cleared his throat.

"It is the finding of this committee that, in view of his family's history with this institution, Mr. Robert Clarke will NOT be expelled from this club. He will however attend several sensitivity sessions to be overseen by Mr. Siddiqi, who on behalf of this great country of immigrants and multiculturalism, has designed a way to the light for the non-believer and former Crusader."

He then wiped his brow and sat down with a thud. The stringy woman at the end of the head table who was head of the women's squash section moved to declare the meeting over, as her tight schedule precluded any more foolishness. Sheila Sharpe was her name, and in spite of her tight schedule, she took the time to berate me on behalf of the women's section, women in general and most assuredly liberal intellectuals everywhere.

Her motion was met with enthusiasm, whereupon everyone left for lunch except Mr. Siddiqi and myself. The delightful yet toothless Mammcreet Nabir was shown the door by the wise Mr. Siddiqi who refused to share a meal with a woman.

I won't drag the dear reader over the following hour of misery that I endured, with a bucket of humus and pita bread washed down, not with the longed for G&T, just bottled water without a label which tasted odd.

The damned Path to Light and Forgiveness was finally explained by the kind Mr. Siddiqi, after he pocketed my cheque, that I was sure was supposed to go to the absent Mammcreet and her wretched husband for that trip, and after he had eaten an alarming amount of the frightful humus, which I, as I don't trust foreign rubbish, just picked at it.

The Path consisted of turning up at the old mosque and having a chinwag with the Imam or something.

What did I care, a few words and then with a yank of the beard and I am back sitting in my usual chair at the club. So with a light heart on the following Thursday night I made my way to the address mentioned on the handy paper Mr. Siddiqi had provided, a lot of Sanskrit and an odd looking chap in a beard on the other side. I don't know why they have to build their bloody mosques in cow fields well out of the city, as it took forever to arrive. I raced up to the brightly lit temple, Temple? I thought it was called a mosque, oh well lets not stand on ceremony, lets get the bloody groveling out of the way and return to the club. I shot inside to be confronted by bearded men not pleased to see me and I could tell this by the two turbaned chaps who began to strangle me. Apparently I put up a bit of a struggle or at least that is what a very pleasant woman with a promising figure told me after I had regained consciousness in an antechamber of the temple. It was she who rescued me from those villains by the door. I can't for the life of me remember what this dear woman's name was for she was unable to tell me that or her phone number as 3 men with scimitars approached me and one of them was her husband. It turned out, after a very surly gentleman explained, that one did not enter a Sikh temple without a hankie on one's head. Sikh temple!!!! Wrong place, wrong religion. So I took my leave as new thinking Sikhs began to have chairs thrown at them by the more orthodox, and everyone seemed delighted. I can take this religion game or not, but everyone seems so martial.

You can say what you want about us Anglicans, all we can think of after the last hymn is the Sunday roast and a large ginsy, not throwing chairs at one another.

With new directions from my one female contact with the fierce Sikhs, I made my way up what seemed a farmer's road until after crossing a bridge; an enormous building loomed out of the darkness. They don't seem to scrimp on money these chaps, my God it was huge, and it must put the cows off their milk having something like that looking at you as you try to graze. I had to park at the far end of the bloody lot as it was packed with every known make and model of vehicle.

Trudging through the snow I began to feel not a little sorry for myself and with good reason. I had been caught up in a cultural quagmire because a bloody woman, from overseas somewhere, had strolled out of the bloody loo which by the way could have very well given ME a stroke, and the upshot is I am pilloried. My name according to the bartender at the National Club on Bay Street, has even been seen in the gutter press, and what did I do? Muttering to myself in the cold night as I made my way towards the monstrosity of a building, I noticed the form of the ever vigil Mr. Siddiqi, standing on the steps. He suddenly became very animated as I approached.

"Where have you been O Crusader/Infidel…Shame, shame! "? This was the first time that I had heard him work both of those terms into the same sentence. It was impressive.

"Sorry O Effendi, I was lost and now I am found. " as I tried to work a little of the old bible into the conversation. Why must there only be tolerance on one side of the issue. Meanwhile I was seriously becoming frozen standing on those cold marble steps, why couldn't we go in for heaven's sake? But the man Siddiqi wasn't having any of it.

"O unbeliever you mock me, you mock the Prophet and you are late!" he roared, so close to me that I could make out the recently eaten humus between his teeth. Which is ironic as it was a little something in my teeth that put me in this mess in the first place. If I were not so hygienic and caring I would not have bothered making that historic trip to the Men's john. Sigh. It troubles me still, the memory I carry of the next almost three hours, God's teeth it was stultifying boredom by

anyone's barometer. I put my head down and went in. Two
other followers of Siddiqi escorted me into the main room
of the mosque, while placing one of those round hats onto
my shiny cranium. I momentarily cheered up when I saw all
those bums in the air, perhaps I would be facing a nice big
lady's behind. Not a bit of it as women seem to be segregated
to some other part of the mosque, which meant I had some
man's, and in fact many men's rear quarters facing me. Please
Lord, no gas. As the reader knows I am a great believer in
women, the more the merrier and all that, what is it with these
people, do they not want females around or what. 50% of
their community is not allowed to pray with the other half.
The prophet had nine wives so he clearly wanted girls around.
These thoughts were all for naught as the Imam begun to get
stuck into his sermon, although not in English. It has been in
my short stay among these believers an obvious truism that
the term "Sense of Humour" remains a mystery and certainly
this chap at the lectern was not a happy Boy Scout. He began
by shouting and went from there on up. I thought I had come
upon an opera in its final stages, but as he went from crescendo
to crescendo, I feared for his sanity. I looked around at the
crowd and this clearly is what they had come for, this was the
meat and potatoes served well done. I nervously noticed that
the crowd once or twice turned to look at me in reference to
what the big guy was saying. He pointed at me a few times and
shook his fist many times as I tried to put on the face of the
Angel Gabriel, who seems to have been very busy amongst the
religions of those times. Finally, finally it ended. If you think
at my age I enjoyed squatting on that floor you're mad. I could
hardly get to my feet. I struggled upright only to be grabbed
by the original gentlemen who brought me in, which now
removed me back from whence I came, namely the front door.
What a night not a woman in sight and everyone scowling at
me, in fact not much of an advertisement for said religion.
Where's the fun? You would have been proud of me though as

I kept my tongue in my head, shook hands with those bloody people and bolted for home and a new start at the club. I vowed never to return to any other sensitivity sessions, nor did the wise Mr. Siddiqi ask me.

CHAPTER 10

(Molly comes into Robert's life and may have damaged him for life. Ed)

Molly Reuvan. That name still chimes for me, even after some fifty years or so. Julian Reuvan was a master at Crescent during my fourth form year and was much loved by our year. In Grade Four Mr. Reuvan was teaching us Greek and Latin, while three years before I had been learning "See Spot run." Anyone who doesn't see the difference between public and private school is barking mad. Of course if you don't want to think of your child being thrashed, perhaps public school is for you and yours.

Mr. Reuvan could best be described as an aesthete on his way to martyrdom. He would bring a flower to class and stare at it for hours as we conjugated and declined our way through the textbooks in front of us. Eventually putting his flower on the window sill, he make his way to his desk at the front of the class while looking out over our heads in a dreamy way, saying something like, "Consider, boys, the saints as they lived and died, lo those many years ago. Torn asunder for their beliefs and faith, eaten alive by beasts, crucified as our Lord was, with great fear and yet conviction, the conviction of who they were and what they believed in." He spoke these words softly but with the kind of English accent that made it all seem so real.

As I write this, I cannot help but remember that today is St Andrew's Day and the teachings of Mr. R. flood back upon me. St. Andrew was crucified on an X-shaped cross in Greece about 60 AD. Now that is an education you can use. We certainly did with Laverty at recess. We held him down to see whether he could be crucified on an X. Beamish, whose father owned a construction firm, reckoned they must have broken St. Andrew's legs to make it work properly. Just then Laverty bolted for sanctuary back at the school. As a matter of record, it took four days for St. Andrew to die on his odd cross, but I have forgotten why Scotland's flag has the cross of St. Andrew, also known as the Saltire cross.

What a teacher Mr. Reuvan was! No teachers' unions for him, no guaranteed pension, no touchy-feely nonsense, just his strength of character and his sense of the dramatic. Every day he would fill our little heads with exciting events and human courage so that we could discuss nothing else with our friends or parents. My mother was quite sickened as I described at dinner one night (when I was not boarding at school) the careful breaking of bones that certain Christians had to endure. Father, on cue, snapped a turkey leg in two.

I can see Mr. Reuvan to this day, a tall but stooped man with overlong straight black hair that flew about as he shook with passion during the telling of great slaughters. Long nose, with the skin around his face stretched across the bones. An Adam's apple that was a metronome for his moods in a neck that went snaking into a frayed English shirt. He had a look of utter melancholy, as if he had seen and lived a thousand lives. He had been a commando with the SAS in the Second World War and had seen sights and done things that were only hinted at.

This wounded man washed up on the shore of Crescent with his quiet wife and their daughter Molly. Molly was not unlike Mademoiselle George, the actress during the reign of Napoleon Bonaparte 1, who at the ripe age of fifteen took

Paris by storm, the Nell Gwyn of her day. Not only was she a superb actress but she also bedded all who mattered in her era, starting with Napoleon himself and Talleyrand and completing the circle with the Duke of Wellington after Waterloo, whom she described as "plus fort" in comparison to the brooding Emperor.

Let me describe Mr. Reuvan's red-headed daughter from the perspective of a smitten ten-year-old. Molly was almost fourteen that winter. Her eyes were the obligatory blue but a new blue, a softer and truer blue while her skin was awash with tiny freckles on a white canvas. Molly stood 5 foot 6, and she smiled as if she knew she could bring down governments via her beauty. Her waist and hips seemed to move on separate hinges as if she were a young Sophia Loren. Her body shaped as if all others were askew and only hers was perfect. She was the most desirable creature I would ever know. In short she was perfect.

If I am slightly off centre today, it is due to the sight of Molly at such an early age. Why not? If a child is shocked when very young it seems perfectly reasonable to make note of it. And what about all that latent memory foolishness, "Oh yes, Doctor, I had somehow forgotten that my father tried to diddle me at six." Stuff and nonsense. I remember Molly all too well and if she had told me to butcher the headmaster it would have been but the work of a moment.

It was the following spring when it happened. My parents had decided to resume their cruise at the Easter holidays, so after sixteen months of being a day boy — brought to school each day by a Metro taxi — they stuck me back in the dorms. It was the beginning of spring and my sap was running, although I am not sure I knew what that meant.

The only blight on the horizon was that dear Matron had fallen for a certain Mr. Barry, the music master, who was also my house master at Hudson House and a popular man. I was delighted with her choice but understood that my days of clinging to her perfect legs had come to an end. There was one last small moment of play between us all, and that came about because I was slow in exiting the showers one night. Mr. Barry, who by then spent all his time up on the third floor, chased me down the hallway towards Manchester dorm and as I turned into doorway he flicked me with a wet towel and caught me square on Sebastian. There was the sound of an enormous crack and then I was down, rolling in pain, to the joy of my dorm mates.

Mr. Barry turned white and carried me down the hall to the infirmary. After much fussing by both Matron and Mr. Barry, it was concluded to be nothing more than a flesh wound. What a cheek! I said nothing, just looked at them as they giggled and frolicked as the lovebirds they were. In the end, and it only seems odd now, they put a tongue depressor on each side of the outraged Sebastian as a splint, followed by much talk of what should hold the splint together. There I was lying on a cot in the infirmary with my pajamas down to my ankles and these two fussing over my loins as I looked on like a slightly interested third party. In today's world there would have been hell to pay, with the school being sued by every boarder and me being mined for repressed memory or some other BS. If the truth were known I was more impressed with way matron handled my block and tackle than Mr. Barry, who seemed to regard my manhood with only passing regard and little gentleness.

I was sometimes shocked by Mr. Reuvan's passion for poetry. He could often be found at the stream that ran through the lower field, weeping over his book of verse. Oscar Wilde once said about the death of Nell, "You would have to have a heart of stone not to laugh." In Mr. Reuvan, we had the opposite. He would cry at the sight of a swallow or a purring cat. Matron said he felt so lucky to be alive after the war that he couldn't help it.

We first met Molly when her father brought her mother and her to a hymn service in the great hall of the school near Christmas. All we boys knew about his family was that he had one child and that they lived in a dreadful row housing adjacent to the front gates of the school property. It was what my father would have called "the type of shabby housing that should be leveled and the builder hung". But from all sources they were extremely happy to be in their new country.

At the point in the service where the headmaster leads his staff and their families into the hall, Kennedy stuck his finger into my ribs. "Bloody hell, look at her, Clarke," he said. He did not have to tell me twice. The entire school body swiveled their necks as one to look at a perfect redhead with the softly freckled face. She took this mass adoration as her due.

I have no other recollection of the hymn service except the burning in my soul for Molly Reuvan. She began to spend time with the boarders and our world brightened enormously. Often she would accompany her father to the school and while he wept in the gardens she would frolic with us in the upper fields by the old stables. Molly would send us on scavenger hunts that were extraordinary. She would insist that her word was was law to her "worker bees," as she called us, and she was our Queen. We loved her en masse.

She would sit us down in the high grass of the middle meadow and give us our orders.

"Well, boys, it's a fine afternoon," she would start, sitting in front of us in a short skirt with her panties clearly visible, "with every promise of a jolly scavenger hunt ahead." We said nothing. Our eyes were locked onto her white underwear.

"Now we all remember the tale of St. Fridiswede, the patron saint of Oxford," she said. It was just like her father's classes. We stared dumbly back at her, having no idea who St. Fridiswede was.

She sighed but continued, "In order to preserve her virginity she fled to Oxford and started a convent, you silly boys." None of us were too sure what virginity was, but we liked being referred to as silly boys. Her voice was like that of the actress Debra Kerr, well bred, but with something beneath. She adjusted her sitting position by shooting her long legs into the air over our heads and then inclining her body towards us.

"Well, I am not bloody St. Fridiswede and this is not bloody Oxford, so I want you to go over that river and fetch me all the 'smalls' you can find on those laundry lines I can see from here."

Oh, Lord, we thought as we looked at each other. Those lines were on the surrounding properties outside school bounds. "Excuse me, Miss," I ventured, "We are not allowed off school property. It is a strapping offense." I was encouraged by the nodding heads of the other boarders.

Morgan piped up, "And what are 'smalls,' Miss?" I was glad Morgan asked that and not me, as the Clarke courage was not very developed yet. She eyed him for a moment and then said, "You brave little boy, come to me." Morgan looked at us, then back at Molly, and was torn by indecision.

"Morgan," she said softy. At the sound of his name coming from those lips Morgan broke the sitting high-jump record and landed beside her. I began to realize that through hesitation I had missed my chance to be favoured as Morgan now was.

"These are smalls," she said, and slowly spread her legs. We gaped at what today would be described as "sport shorts." They were bright white and loose fitting, not at all the current idea of eroticism, but to us they were delightful. Morgan had the best view while the rest of us strained our optic nerves to the breaking point. After looking at each one of us, she slowly closed her legs and stood up.

"I will give you another show, you little bleeders, after you scavenge those clotheslines," she said roughly. We needed no further inducements. We circled her once as a gathering flock and then tore off in the direction of her pointing finger. We weren't terribly sure what we had seen between those legs, but one thing was certain: We wanted more.

Perhaps it was the fact we were all dressed the same with our school sweaters and grey shorts that gave away our home base. Let's just say the cause was not helped by a besotted Morgan running past a shocked housewife holding at least ten of her neighbours' bras shouting, "Crescent for ever and long live Queen Molly."

Within the hour Mr. Williams had been awakened from his Saturday afternoon nap by outraged homeowners suggesting that the residence of the current Lord of the Flies gang should have a good dose of socialism with the place torn down, mass hangings and affordable housing erected in its stead.

When we reached the crest of the hill leading down to the school we couldn't find Molly, but we could make out the tiny figure of the headmaster doing what looked like some sort of two-step dance on the circular driveway. We watched as the poor man leapt about, with only the sound of a distant cough coming our way. Morgan suggested it was not the time to reveal our bounty to Mr. Williams, and perhaps a quick burial was needed. We returned to the forest and set about preparing a safe repository for our treasure. It was clear even to us that we had stripped the nearby community of every type of form-fitting suspension known to man. Hixson alone had collected more than twenty bras and not a few girdles with several huge men's underwear, of which many were torn.

As we looked at it, it became evident that the pile was too large for any hole we could possibly dig in the next few minutes. Once again the brain of Ramsey minimus came to the fore. "We shall put them into the trees," he said in a rather Churchillian manner.

"Brilliant!" we shouted together and set about our work. At the start we gently placed the girdles and bras on the lower boughs, laying them flat so the first tree took on the look of a freethinking department store. However Morgan, our lookout, reported that the head had been joined by others who were about to spread out in what looked to Morgan like some sort of unenlightened posse.

The department store look was abandoned for the newer approach of flinging whatever was at hand into whichever tree was closest. We spread out as each tree became cluttered, until the forest began to look like the last stop before a well-attended nudist camp. The larger clothing rose higher into the trees, as the air seemed to lift those items with ease, whilst those of the thinner populace took the lower bunks. We faced what surely would be our martyrdom at the hands of the now anabolizing Mr. Williams. I recalled Mr. Reuvan's stories of the saints who had suffered. Close to home there was the redoubtable John de Brébeuf, a Jesuit who had baptized more than 7,000 Hurons in Quebec and Ontario between 1629 and 1649. The Iroquois caught up to him in 1649 and made him and his pals pay for their beliefs. Beaten with clubs, and then baptized in boiling water, they had their skin removed with white-hot tomahawks and eaten. Or perhaps John Forrest, who in 1538 was cooked slowly over a green fire at Smithfield in London. We trudged gloomily back to the school and the torture preceding our certain deaths.

The long and the short of it all was that we were summarily strapped, which almost killed Mr. Williams, as there were twelve of us to be beaten with twelve strokes on each hand — twenty-four strokes for each boy or 288 strokes altogether. The last three boys had their strapping done by a prostrate headmaster from his ancient couch. Unfortunately I was the second in line and so got to feel the rage gripping the shouting Headmaster:

"I might have known, Clarke, that you would be a leader in this Ali-Baba throng. Gone quiet, have you, boy? (Cough, cough) I will soon bring sounds from your cheeky lips (cough, cough)!" And he did. For a weak man he fairly jumped with delight as he brought the strap down upon my shaking hand.

"Hold still, you wretched rodent, or it will go all the worse for you. Bloody family, I did the same to your father with little result. I shall try harder with you, my boy!" With that he started to use both his hands on the handle, which gave the descending leather a new and alarming velocity. The tool of torture sang through the air as I stood and inwardly wept, for I was too old now, in school terms, to show weakness and cry. So I thought of Molly's smalls and got through the ordeal. My only joy was that he miscounted and tried to give one extra, but I had naturally already lowered my throbbing hands so that he brought the strap down on his own thin thigh. Mr. Williams beet-red danced with a flurry of yelps and jumps but dismissed me with a wave as a new victim stepped forward.

That was not the only thing required of us for our misdeeds. We were made to go back to the now "fully Marxist" neighbourhood and present letters of apology to one and all as well as retrieve the stolen articles. That bit about the "articles" was a bit rough as the garments had been in the forest for almost two days, one of which had had rain, so there would be no tea and crumpets served to us in gratitude. We were met by, I thought, a surly crowd that didn't seem at all mollified by our quickly written and rather form-like letters.

"What did you think you were doing?" said one of the brighter-looking neighbours. I began to see the fox's point of view as far as the so-called fun of being hounded. The men and boys with some of the larger women surrounded us in their enthusiasm over finally getting at us. I did, however, think I spotted the woman whose triple D bra had floated the highest.

That happy thought was dashed from my head as one woman screamed at us, "Do you have any idea what it is like to come out to your line and find ALL your girdles missing?"

Our position was thoroughly undermined by Morgan shouting back, "No, Madam, I can't say as I do, never having needed one." Morgan's retort went down in school history, and is something I am often asked to recall, as Morgan is no longer in the land of the living, having been run over by a less than amused husband in later years. He was still under the influence of Molly at the time.

A huge man stepped forward, rolling up his sleeves. "You speak to my dear wife like that?" he asked. This is it, I thought. Just then the hulking figure of Mr. Noonan swam into view. Several of the lower classes of the neighbourhood shrank back at his presence, even as the unhappy husband assessed his chances. Mr. Noonan had a large smile on his face as he spoke soothingly to the man, "You are quite right sir, these boys need a lesson, and I'm just the person to give it to them."

"I would hope you will, my man," said the relieved villager, for Mr. Noonan was wearing his usual gym shirt, which stretched painfully across his enormous chest, leaving no doubt what would be the outcome of any contretemps. Mr. Noonan continued pleasantly, "I think a taste of the lash is what is called for, don't you?" The serfs nodded dumbly, although we noticed that a few of the children looked sympathetically in our direction.

Mr. Noonan then grabbed the nearest boy, Morgan, by the ear, saying, "Come with me, you little Jacobites," and off we marched towards the school, with a few of the local children following. Morgan danced along beside Mr. Noonan begging for mercy, but the master was having none of it. When eventually we came within sight of the Upper School and the locals had been seen off, Mr. Noonan let go of Morgan's crimson ear and stopped to look at us.

"There is the last of it, boys, well done and don't do it again," he smiled. "You'll not forget today soon, will ye? " We all smiled back at him. "Right, I'll race you to the school doors and the one who beats big Jack Noonan will have a butter tart for sure," and he was off, running swiftly for such a large man. We gathered our wits and shot after him. He was the first man not of fiction or history that I wished to emulate, and I hope he is well, wherever he is.

We hadn't seen Molly for a few weeks and assumed she was on to more sophisticated adventures. We did have fun ribbing Morgan, who kept calling for Molly and her "smalls" while he slept. We even took a wet washcloth and laid it over his toes as he slept and shortly we were rewarded with the sight of Morgan peeing straight up into the air and wetting his bed. He was gated for two weeks by Mr. Barry for gross indecency towards his dear Matron.

One day just before the Easter holidays, Molly reappeared. Her father was doing his depressed poet routine at the window when there was a soft knock on the fourth form door and Molly walked back into our yearning lives. She blessed us with her smile and then looked fondly over to her father. "Daddy," she said, "Mummy wishes to know whether you will be home for tea tonight."

"What's for tea, my lovely?" inquired the master, and our heads swiveled back to Boadicea, which is what we secretly referred to her as after the village incident. Boadicea was the widow of Prasutagus, king of the Iceni, who after being raped by Roman soldiers led that famous rebellion in 61 AD. She sacked the Roman cities of London, Colchester and St. Albans and gave no quarter before being defeated. She committed suicide by poison shortly thereafter.

"Bangers and mash, Daddy," she trilled.

"Cor, brilliant. Tell Mummy I shan't be long," came the reply. Molly once again favoured each of us with her blue eyes and gently closed the door.

We had understood most of what they had said to each other. "Tea" meant supper and "bangers and mash" meant sausages in a baked pie made up of mashed potato. But "cor"? Morgan came to our rescue with his large book of Chums, which he received six times a year from a maiden aunt in Cornwall. He found a passage that mentioned a policeman or "bobby," named for the first police chief, who spotted a nice-looking widow bending down to pick up her hat and uttered the phrase, "Cor, lovely!" Why would our master say that about his daughter? Hixson supposed it was anything that was nice, as in the "bangers and mash." We accepted that.

The holidays meant most boarders returned home for ten days, but there were always a few that were left at the school — we were called "the Lepers." That year in the dorm was a fat kid from the Yukon, who everyone believed was rich from the gold rush but was in fact a deacon's son whose tuition was paid by kindly parishioners. He was in Grade Nine (or the sixth form as it was called there) and therefore a senior boy. There were two lads from China whose parents were missionaries and hadn't been heard from for years. We took great delight in telling them savages had eaten their parents. Mr. Williams strapped five of us for frightening them.

Notman, who was in the fourth with me, had low blood pressure and hence would pass out often from little frights. His parents had divorced, which was shocking in the early 1950s, and neither was fighting over him. And then there was Hand from Bermuda, who cured me forever of trying to bully anyone. My father would refer to someone of Hand's colouring as "a touch of the tar brush," and we called him Chocolate Boy. He was good at cricket so we liked him in the spring, but he was useless at hockey. One winter's day I was laughing at his struggles on the ice rink along with the others, and he decided to put an end to it. Once changed from his hockey gear, he sought me out. I was standing by the tuck shop near the basement corridor when he came upon me.

"The next time you call me Chocolate Boy, you will regret it, Clarke," he said. He had challenged me in front of my friends. What could I do?

"Eh, Chocolate Boy?" I said. Then he struck me full in the mouth. It was so quick I was not sure what had happened. My friends piled onto him and beat him into submission, but

I have the chipped tooth to this day as a reminder of my days as a bully. Hand and I became not fast friends but at least respectful of each other.

There was one other poor little chap, Eckert, who had some sort of skin irritation that kept him encased in fearful lotions and indoors most of the time, so some unkind boys pointed out that we really were lepers with Eckert in our midst.

On the last day of school I watched as my friends' parents in their swank cars swept into the courtyard to retrieve their sons. I waved goodbye to Laverty, Hixson and Morgan from my dorm window three stories above the happy scene. Matron told me my cruising parents were just coming into sight of Cyprus and sadly couldn't be with me over Easter. I felt very alone. I suppose it can't have been much fun for the masters, stuck looking after us through Easter, but somehow that did not occur to me till I was well into my thirties. Back then it was my own forlornness that counted.

The first few days were cold and rainy and we were confined to barracks, so most of the time was taken up with reading history and such. The food was, if possible, more appalling than usual as there were fewer witnesses to the spectacle of five or six boarders gagging on their turnips, brussels sprouts and parsnips. The hairy dietitian was providing for her pension by not feeding us properly, stealing the funds that were set aside to make our stay as pleasant as possible. During the year, every Thursday in our geography lesson near the kitchen doors, we could make out the odours of those three terrible vegetables and our hearts sank.

I know I am drifting a bit here but I have to keep explaining the everyday workings of dear old Crescent. I will return to the holiday break shortly

Thursday was the most hated day of the week not only because of that, but because it was also the day Mr. Williams beat the boys with six demerits or more. It was an honour system without honour. Any master could give a boy a demerit for offenses from filthy words to filthy habits. "Take a demerit Clarke" still rings in my ears from far ago. The master would take out a 3x4 blue card and write the misdemeanor and the number of demerits being given. The student then was honour bound to deposit the demerit card into a large box outside the dining room. I was continually thrashed for trying to flush the blasted things down the toilet.

"Clarke, you have done untold damage to the cistern, you awful boy (cough, cough)," Mr. Williams would scream as he hit me. "So like your father, boy," he continued. One of the reasons I received so many demerits was that I refused to eat the three veg on Thursdays. God, I hated them and I have never eaten any of them since. More than one girl's family has been shocked as I left the house, saying, "I wouldn't eat them at school and I am certainly not eating them now."

The point I was trying to make was, Easter appeared to be like the rest of the year only worse, but my lifelong optimism had its roots in that holiday.

Molly came to lunch by herself that Thursday, and with a hearty "Hello, my young knights, how are we today?" she announced that she would be at the school for the rest of Easter. Our hearts sang. The hairy dietitian wanted to know whether this meant more food was required. In answer Molly simply dropped a note from the head onto the table, telling one and all that Molly would be standing in for various masters as supervisor for the rest of the holidays. Molly turned to us and smiled. "And we shall have such a brilliant time, shan't we, boys?"

"Hooray!" we shouted together.

Molly then turned back to the hairy dietitian and asked her to please in the future at least the near future to refrain from cooking those particular veg.

Molly had joined us just as the sun started to shine on what became known as the hottest Easter ever in eastern North America. It blistered us for eight glorious days. The first thing that happened (you will have to forgive me as I adjust the block and tackle while writing this passage in the library of the club) was that Molly decided we could all frolic together in our "smalls." We were so excited after she had told us this at tea that we could hardly settle down to sleep in anticipation of the next day. Matron and Mr. Barry returned from their daily sojourns and were annoyed at the disturbance. We just giggled into our pillows.

We were up earlier than usual, wearing our usual thick woolen short trousers with the mandatory high woolen socks and white short-sleeved gym shirts. This was known as boarder spring dress and was inspected by Matron every morning just as it would have been if school were still in. We lined up dutifully for our spoonful of cod liver oil. Most of the boys hated this ritual, so that there was always a master present in case corporal punishment was needed to make the more recalcitrant to do their duty. I loved the stuff and was usually first in line, having peed in the sink to save time and so get the clean spoon and the first of the nectar. I would sometimes go to the rear of the line to try for another and ask for a new spoon.

Even those who hated the fish oil got it down without gagging that morning, then ran down the circular back stairs for breakfast. Molly was sitting there waiting for us, but the two missionary kids purloined the nearest seats to her, so we had to be content with spitting in their runny eggs. The dietitian poked her head through the swinging doors that led to the kitchen. She must have heard our chortling, for her head shot back and she fixed us with a stern look usually saved for one of the workers about to dispose of four-day-old Spam. We didn't care — we only had eyes and ears for Molly.

The next few days were all about learning such games as British Bulldog, Flags and Treasure Island, which consisted of finding buried spoils thanks to maps Molly provided. These were halcyon times, and we were all in our underwear. I am not sure what we must have looked like running across fields in our over-laundered Y fronts, as Molly called them. My poor excuses for undergarments were by the start of the third term almost grey with no working elastic left. There was something else we all shared; our underwear had become shapeless, so that when we ran there was every possibility that one or two testicles could be seen peeking from their rookeries. Molly never brought attention to our shortcomings, so that after a day or two when sitting in a semi-circle around her awaiting new instructions, we would only make cursory attempts at replacing the free-thinking appendages in their perches. There were the occasional injuries, however, especially whilst playing British Bulldog, where the object of the game was not to get killed. The good news for the injured was a cuddle with Molly, which quickly became abused as those damn missionary kids started falling over during map reading. They were the worst kind of brown-nosers, but there was nothing we could do without a nod from Molly.

I come now to Molly's greatest moment. Remember that Molly was also in her smalls and even as the years fall away, there has never been a sight like that. Her panties were the kind that was so prevalent then, rising almost to her belly button with looseness around the hips. Her bra was sensible and covered most of her breasts, but still Molly looked like nothing else on earth. With the waning light we would march back towards the school, finding our clothes where we had hidden them by the tree near the rose garden, with erections on one and all. Molly could not have missed this fact but said nothing.

On the last evening before the return of the other boarders, Molly seemed in no hurry to break up our companionship, although she would normally have headed off home. Instead she was looking conspiratorial.

"Come on, you lot, I will walk you back to school. Knowing you, I'll get blamed for you getting lost," she said. We, of course, were happy to have as much time with her as possible in these last few hours. We followed her back to the courtyard, but not the well- trod way, but by a circuitous route, staying close to the stream till we were below the balustrades of the courtyard driveway and then straight up the walls of the ravine till we were just under the overhang of the car parking lot beside the back door.

"Right, my knights, be quiet and follow me, mind, not a sound now," and she stepped through bracken to a secret staircase, and a very old door leading into the school. This was exciting. We roamed freely everywhere on the school property but we had never seen this before. Molly led us through back tunnels of the inner boiler rooms below the pool, an area I don't think any student had seen up until then.

Hand paused, saying, "How did you know about this?" Molly just rubbed her nose with her finger, which I learned later meant it was a secret. She was hunching over as the ceiling came down to meet us in the form of huge round pipes. Suddenly she stopped, straightened up and led us into a small round room about eight feet in circumference with a single light dead above the centre of the room. Molly stood in the middle over what looked like a drain and we formed a semi-circle around her and waited. One of the missionary kids asked, "What time's our tea?" but no one answered because something was going to happen, something that Molly had planned, and our mouths were dry as cardboard.

"Boys, this is the room where the Masseys tested water and milk and other things before pasteurization took hold. This is where doctors looked at sick people too, see the drains? They were so afraid of sickness that they had this isolation room to make sure the disease didn't spread. The man died anyway. But that's not why we are here. This is our last night before the boarders return, and in two days the last term of the year begins. Let's be honest now, my boys, we shan't see each other again really, not like it's been."

We looked around at each other and Notman nodded. Molly looked at each one of us sadly. "None of us know what will become of each other or of ourselves for that matter, so we must remember our time when we were young and free and had no worries. So remember this!" she shouted and stepped out of her clothes and stood naked before us. Notman immediately fainted but claimed later to have heard everything. The rest of us hardly breathed as we looked at her perfect beauty. Molly watched us as we pored over her flawless white freckled body. We pondered her and she us, with just the laboured breathing and swelling of our chests. She was as excited as we were and that in turn made for even more stimulation. We boys had no clue what to do, so we just looked.

She seemed to understand our excitement and she deemed us worthy, her good servants, as we never told on her for the incident with the bras and girdles. Minute after minute passed and we could not turn away. She had very long legs, which would reveal her thigh muscles when she flexed, a high perfect bum tapering to a smallish waist but not thin. Her bosoms were a triumph for when she had removed her rather severe bra, they actually rose up. Her reddish hair framed the bluest of eyes, eyes that illuminated the dark corners of your mind. In short she understood us all and in her future all men.

Finally the kid with the lotion started to cry, which broke the spell, and Molly was dressed in a flash. It was over. But everything was different now. And as I stare from my chair at the club near the top of the stairs at the young girls passing on their way to the squash section, I can see Molly still.

CHAPTER 11

(The unpleasant incident at camp and the last of Molly Reuvan.)

We saw Molly once more at Prize Day near the end of term. With my long missing parents in attendance it was tough to get near her, but I had to. I broke away when I won the Religious Award for my house (Hudson). As I came down the stairs, Molly was sitting to the right of the stage. I ran over to her and in front of her stunned parents and the entire school, I blurted out, "Let's get married, I love you!" The school body had a good laugh at that, but Molly rose quickly and embraced me, saying, "My brave knight, I will wait for you." That stopped my friends' laughter and I sat down beside my father to general applause.

My mother was outraged by my behaviour, and I could see Mr. Williams wishing he could have a moment of my time in his office, but my father seemed to look upon me with a newfound respect from one man to another. "She's a bit of all right, eh?" he said happily. I said nothing in return, for I knew I would never see Molly again.

The summer began with the news that Mr. Williams had died in harness at the final board of directors meeting. He had risen on a point of order to oppose a motion to limit the amount of smoking allowed in the school because of the high cost of insurance. Mr. Williams shouted, "It does no harm as far as I am concerned" and then died. He was 78.

At camp I was still infused with the spirit of Molly and moped around for the first week or so, but my older sister Jane, who was a counsellor in training, would have none of it and drew me out of myself.

The place was called Camp Gay Venture and it still well may be, but I'll bet there is a lot of laughter about the name now. It was a co-ed camp, but boys were only allowed to stay till they were twelve while the girls carried on to sixteen. It was felt the boys would become too unruly after twelve to let them mingle with girls. I was turning ten that summer and all I had to look forward to was Mr. Prig in the Shell or fifth form. What a thought.

I noticed straightaway that I was much more interested in girls than my other tent-mates, all because of Molly, I guess. The camp uniform of those days was a short-sleeved T-shirt and shorts in Sherwood Forest green. The girls' shorts were very short, in fact Americans referred to them as Canadian shorts or short shorts. This was a pleasant change for a boy locked up in a dorm. The camp was based on getting everyone as fit as possible with good food and not a hairy dietitian in sight. I loved it. The boys were kept separate from the girls' quarters, which surrounded our tents in the middle. There were many more girls than boys and the girls looked at us as experiments that had gone bad. We accepted that and had fun amongst ourselves anyway canoeing, riding, sailing and swimming.

One day I saw my sister talking to a small group of the older girls at the docks. Jane was a good swimmer and took only the best for her advanced swimming class, which she ruled with an iron fist. The girls loved her and listened raptly to every word. I waved at my sister in passing, whereupon she tried to kick me. I easily dodged her foot but couldn't help noticing the smallest of the group, Wendy. I had an instant crush. She was blonde, not unlike a smaller version of Miss Peacock, and slim with a pretty chest, an upturned nose above her full lips and the greenest eyes possible. She may not have been a Molly but I was pole-axed Again.

The boys ate in the middle of the Great Cabin and the girls on either side. Wendy sat three tables away on my right, and if I managed to get the end seat I would be looking straight at my new love. She wasn't Molly, but since there could never be another of her, one had to make do. Besides I had the bug. I had had to share Molly with those halfwits from the dorm, but I didn't have to share Wendy.

I clearly could not to tell my sister anything as she might feel her position as counsellor in training could be jeopardized. In addition, she was pretending she was French, walking around with a stupid accent because of Jacques, a dish hog in the kitchen whom she was "in like with", as they said in those days. I didn't tell any of my tent-mates either. I really only could abide two of them but they weren't boarders at their schools and so would not understand the concept of keeping secrets, which was life or death to a boarder. Each day I would hurl a winning smile at Wendy as we ate, and each day she would nod back in what I took to be a fond way. Things seemed to be moving along well.

My swimming had improved thanks to being able to swim all year at school. The camp owners checked my ability in the water carefully now. That was because in my first year I had given everyone a bit of a fright. I was six then and I had taken a fair amount of gym from my sister and her instructor in Toronto so I had no fear of flips, front or back. When I arrived at camp they asked each of us "new things" whether we could swim and dive, and not hearing the owner properly I thought he said swim or dive, so I put up my hand. They were delighted to have someone so young as a possible diver, which is what I said I was, as I certainly couldn't swim.

On the second day we potential recruits assembled by the diving tower on the large dock to wait our turn. My sister, who knew of my lack of prowess in the water, was on a camping trip, so I just stood mutely till it was my turn. "Just show me an easy one, no need to overdo it," the female instructor said quietly in my ear. I looked up at the three-metre tower and then looked over at the ladder, the one I would use to climb out of the lake, which was fairly close to where I would enter the water. "OK," I whispered back and scrambled up the steps to my perch.

Usually there was someone called Mr. Cole standing at the end of the box horse to make sure I landed on the mat properly after my springboard jump at Mooredale House, a sort of Gothic rec. centre in Rosedale. I figured I had the height with the tower to make the tuck, so I wouldn't need Mr. Cole at all, and I would just go into the water, find the ladder and crawl up.

The first of the diving each year is a popular occasion for the owners and senior staff members, a chance to see what new talent there was, and how would we do against the other camps. The first few divers had not elicited much enthusiasm, so there was an air of doom settling over the group, as it had the year before with the news that the Brazilian kid was not coming back, he who had singlehandedly won the lake diving two years in a row.

Mr. and Mrs. Ferguson, the owners of Gay Venture, were already writing off this year as well when I ran to the edge, performed a pike with a flip and sailed into the water. I stood on the bottom, looked around, saw the ladder, walked over to it and climbed up. I could hear the noise as I came to the last rung before my head had broken the surface, and being a Clarke, I thought, "Oh oh! My crummy sister must be back." I popped up and stepped onto the dock, only to see two rather large grownups hurtling towards me.

"Well done, my boy!" Mr. Ferguson enthused. "You are just the thing for the camp this year," bellowed Mrs. Ferguson.

And so it was that I came to be the secret weapon for the camp in the competition to be held in two weeks' time, me and some 12-year-old girl from Ohio who had the best teeth I had ever seen and looked like an advertisement for the Chamber of Commerce. We practiced every day and no one ever asked me to swim even a yard or two, just go up and dive from the tower.

The two weeks flew by and the Fergusons were beside themselves with anticipation, as they hoped the judges would love the little boy: me. On Lake Sports Day, there were many guests at Gay Venture, with lots of nearby cottagers, the visiting campers and a few fearful local politicians. And my mother. I saw her pull up in Father's Jag. She had not let me know about this wrinkle, and I began to plan for the worst. Running away was high on my list, so I started packing my rucksack for the speedy flight. Just as I was about to raid Jones's cookie tin for provisions, the diving coach opened the flap to the tent.

"There you are, little Clarke, come and show yourself to the crowds down at the dock," she said. Show myself? Apparently I was some sort of midget weapon the Fergusons wanted to display. She took me by the arm against my protestations and dragged me down to the dock. There was a good crowd and fine weather, two things the camp staff had been praying for, with Mr. Ferguson wiping his brow with his large green hat. Before I knew it the contest was under way, with Camp Gay Venture doing well in the Swimming Winnow competition for seven and under. I could see my mother sitting with the Fergusons, having no idea why she had been given the royal treatment in her son's first year and her daughter off "tripping" somewhere.

The lack of depth in the 12 and unders began to show, with the result the real possibility that our camp could not make the top three for the first time in living memory. Still, to look at the group around the owners and senior staff, one would never think there was an impending disaster. My mother seemed bewildered by it all but occasionally waved in my direction, which only enhanced the bilious feeling moving through my large intestine.

Finally they came to the diving events. If both medals for Boys and Girls could be won by our camp, we stood a chance of finishing well, if not the overall winner. Becky from Ohio didn't have much competition, just a heavyset girl whose dive, unlike Becky's sword-like entry into the lake, soaked both judges and a fair number of the sunburned guests. Becky waved modestly at her proud parents, who had made the 30-hour trip from their home near Cleveland to see their daughter.

It was the Boys' open diving next, and I ambled down to the tower base, trying not to draw attention to myself. I saw my mother looking for me amongst the other contestants in vain. The first boy was from a large camp around the point from Gay Venture, a cocky bunch who all wore the same bathing suits with matching towels. He managed an expert swan dive, and came up grinning beside me as if to say, "Try that, dwarf."

Two other boys dove with varying results, one executing a mediocre foreword flip, the other a disastrous belly flop, to the general hilarity of all except his team, which looked glum. Then I heard it: "Next, Clarke," whereupon my mother stood up. I scrambled up the tower stairs and onto the platform. I looked down at Mother and the Fergusons. Mother seemed to be waving at me with spreading alarm. The whistle blew, telling me to proceed, as I heard my mother say, "But he can't swim a stroke," and then pandemonium broke out.

'What the hell," I thought and did a tight pike with an unexpected twist and a smooth entry into the lake. As I walked towards the ladder I could hear the noise even on the bottom of the lake, and then dozens of bodies hit the water. They damn near drowned me as they fought over who would save me and they upset my tried and true method of getting to the ladder. We all came to the surface spluttering and yelling at the top of our lungs. The camp nurse was attending the two

Fergusons with my mother shouting over them, "This will be a parking lot by the time our lawyers get through with you."

Mother calmed down after a few rye and gingers with the handsome riding instructor and the solemn promise from the Fergusons that mandatory tests of swimming ability would be put in place immediately. There was also hell to pay from the camp association, which banned Gay Venture for two years from entering a competition of any kind.

I return now to Wendy with the dewy lips. I felt our relationship had progressed to the stage of letting her know the extent of my feelings for her; thus I poured my heart out onto two pages of camp stationery that had a little canoe in the top corner. I had a lot of the note paper as it was mandatory to write one's parents twice a week. I had been punished for stuffing my BB targets into an envelope and pretending I had done my duty. Once again my mother had blown the whistle on me and I was cleaning latrines for three days, much to the joy of my sister, whose boyfriend normally had the job.

I told Wendy of the hours when I thought of only her and how the great pine trees looked down upon me in the forest as I walked with her in my heart. I finished it with a flurry about talking to Mr. Raccoon and how he and the other little creatures in the forest approved of our mutual love for each other. Good and meaty stuff, I thought. I shoved it into an envelope and put it at her table with "Wendy" written in green crayon on the front. I almost threw up I was so excited for the lunch to begin. I had images of her coming over to my table, taking me by the hand and walking out, to the applause of one and all.

The lunch bell rang and I shoved my way to the front of the usual queue and waited for the screen doors to open with my stomach doing back-flips. Once the doors were opened, I shot to Wendy's table to make sure my missive was still there, then over to the boys' section, as I scanned the room. I saw her enter with a few of her friends, for she was a popular girl. Oh well, they would have to get along without her soon enough, as I planned that we should be professional campers all year while living in a tree house high above the forest.

She sat down, looked around and saw me staring at her. She raised an eyebrow and gave a questioning smile.

"It will soon be all right, my love." I tried to tell her telepathically. Then she saw the note, which some spotty girl was sniffing at. Just then all the servers entered the hall, blocking any view I had of the proceedings, so I nibbled half-heartedly on the incredibly fresh veg and the largely BBQ'ed meat. Normally I would have tucked in enthusiastically, not today. People always seemed to be standing in front of Wendy, and I couldn't make out her reaction to my letter, although there appeared to be quite a crowd gathered around her table. I wondered if I should go over and share her joy, but I thought waiting would be best.

At the end of these meals, Mr. Ferguson would generally rise and talk about the activities we could look forward to and any points of interest that may have come up. He laboured through the summary and finally said, "Boys and girls, one of the tables would like to read something of interest to all of us." A rushing sound filled my ears, and I watched in dismay as the girl of my, as it turned out, misplaced dreams stood on her table and began to read my love letter in front of the entire camp.

"This is from Robert Clarke," she said. Out of the corner of my eye I saw my sister heading for the screen door. "Every time I see Mr. Beaver and his friend the Eagle, I tell them of my love for you," she read. I could not believe what was happening, Her love for me, where was it? The whole camp began to laugh and point at me as the other boys at my table tried to move away. "But when I see the rippling waters I think of you without clothes on."

"Filth!" shouted Mr. Ferguson, who was an ordained minister. I had only put that bit in to sound more sophisticated.

It went on for a millennium of discomfort and embarrassment, read out with such meanness by my former true love. When she reached the end, where "the squirrels were singing to us", I was getting woozy.

If you wonder why my heart has hardened over the years, here is the core of it. It remains a brightly burning piece of coal consuming my soul. In the end I returned to my cabin alone and despondent. To the shame of my family, I was asked to leave Camp Gay Venture. Sadly Wendy has not a shred of remorse about what she did to me that day. I see her often with her smarmy husband. She doesn't even nod in my direction. I blame my terrible behaviour with poor Ruthy squarely on her beautiful shoulders, damn her.

Fresh hell approached in the shape of Mr. Prig in the fifth form, plus we had a new headmaster, a Mr. Carroll, just off the steamer from England. We didn't get a good look at him until the first assembly and then we got an eyeful. Veins shot off in all directions from his face and jaws, and when we saw his arms, we began to wonder what it would be like to be strapped by this walking sinew. He was tall with a mortarboard on his head and a brightly coloured scarf that was fur-lined, representing university degrees, falling across one shoulder and over his long black cape. When Mr. Carroll clenched his jaw, the veins in his face bulged in protest. He had a beak for a nose and he swiveled his head around as a vulture would at the faint odour of a rotting zebra some distance away. In short he frightened us beyond belief.

The only good news was that Mr. Carroll made Mr. Prig look as frightening as a retired parson on half pay. Whatever Mr. Carroll did at the board of directors' meetings worked, for suddenly new sports equipment arrived, as well as new books that no longer referred to the First World War as the Great War and the War to End All Wars. New classrooms were added and extensions started appearing on both sides of the old school.

Sadly, Mr. Reuvan was gone. We were given no explanation, just that the family had returned to England. What was to become of me?

CHAPTER 12

(This is a hodgepodge of notes and nonsense from Robert. The notes were found in the back of his car but appear to be genuine. Ed)

As exciting as this must seem, I am compelled to return to my roost at the club, for something marvellous happened that I almost forgot to tell you. It says a lot about my character, good, I think. I have just taken another martini as you will appreciate this is thirsty work. You might not think this item is as earth-shattering as I do, however it is my diary and whilst I still breathe I will dictate the direction of it. I must find the name of the new bartender for he certainly knows his way around a martini. Oops, lost it again….Ah, yes, here it comes.

It concerns two pretty squash ladies, I suppose in their mid-thirties or so. I had seen them before, usually surrounded by the young Mountebanks that populate the sports facilities, dreadful cocksure men. Anyway these girls were quite high on the ladder board for the women 40 and under standings. Now I am not making this up, but the really stunning one had been going out of her way to make eye contact with me.

That is not to say that in my day an entrance into the dining room by young Robert Clarke would not be of some interest to the young ladies; indeed the staff often remarked that my presence caused the waiters to pause and not serve any young ladies until I had passed and they had settled down, resuming their dinners. Apparently this habit had arisen because one senior retainer had been badly scalded by the turnip soup he was serving just as a debutante attempted to wave to get my attention. Some unkind souls blamed it on the fact no one likes turnip soup and it shouldn't have been served in the first place. I too despise turnip soup, but I preferred to be the cause, not the soup. Long-ago days.

So imagine my surprise when Melanie, as I came to know her, would go out of her way to give a languid stare and a smile when she passed my chair on the way to the courts. I did the normal thing under the circumstances and checked my fly. I then looked at my old club tie, as my current wife is forever pointing out my inability to get the eggs and bacon all the way to the cake hole, but for once the tie shone brightly back at my enquiry. I had recently been to see Reggie the club barber so that while certainly bald on top,he shaved both sides to give me a harder and leaner and perhaps younger look. But was this enough to hold the interest of such a "looker"?

Each day I arrived precisely at 10 bells, shooed away anyone thinking of settling into my chair, and waited for the opening act to begin. First I would look below me and to the left to watch Melanie enter the club. A flunky would appear to take her overcoat and she would proceed straight ahead to the senior women's dressing room. After a time, she and her friend Alice would saunter out to the squash courts on my right on the second floor, and this is where it would inevitably happen, the long looks, I mean, of the languid variety.

I became more up-tempo in my reactions as time went on, and would be wearing a dazzling smile before she even reached me. This began to unnerve the newer staff who thought I was simply smiling because I was mad as they could not see the target of my happiness. The dessert chef, I think, tried to bring a human rights charge against the club for allowing unmedicated members loose in the upper bar. If I were younger I would have organized a good hiding for the frightful alarmist. In spite of all that Melanie continued in her strange but wonderful habit.

Then one day, just when I thought this was not going to lead to a get-together of any kind, Melanie stopped and asked, "May I sit down, Mr. Clarke?"

I rose to my feet and pointed mutely at the other leather chair. My throat had gone dry. I downed my martini in one but no relief. I pointing madly at my empty vessel, and the waiter returned quickly with the needed tincture. There would be something extra for him under his Christmas tree this year.

Melanie crossed her muscular but shapely legs as she settled into the large chair. At this close distance there was something around the eyes that brought a picture to mind from long ago, but I couldn't remember what it was. I realized I was staring at her in a gormless way, a look that got me caned more than once for gross cheek at school. I pulled myself together and gave Melanie my "keen interest but in your own time, my dear" look.

"Three weeks ago my grandmother died in Florida," she began. I murmured my regrets with the appropriate sympathy. She continued, "I was lucky to have spent so much time with her these past few years, either up here or down at her home by the beach in Fort Myers." Her gin and tonic arrived with another life-restoring martini for me. As the waiter left and I dragged my eyes from my glass I caught her gazing at me in a familiar way.

I don't mind saying that I found it just a little uncomfortable, as if a joke was circulating without my knowledge and I somehow might be the punch line. I took a firmer tone with her. "What's this all about, young lady? I can't but notice that you have been giving me searching looks these past few weeks, and now we are discussing your late grandmother. How may I help you?" That should bring it to a head, I thought. Even in the face of such beauty, we Clarkes can put our foot down.

Melanie looked kindly at me as if she would have to explain to some lost soul the way back to the hospice. We didn't seem to be getting anywhere, so I did what all men in our family do when nonplussed. I stared at my shoes.

Silence, and then an explosion: "She often spoke of you." She beamed.

This sort of thing has happened to me before, some old harpy, embittered and twisted, tries to offload a ton of guilt on me. Well, I am not having it. I have lived my life as best I could with a sharp eye on the Clarke escutcheon and our motto, "Let's try that again, shall we?" which covers almost any circumstance. I remember some dreadful man pulling me close to him as I was entering the club dining room to tell me that his wife had died cursing my name. Normally I would have been happy to listen to his blathering but as this was a Wednesday, which meant roast beef, I was not about to be impeded on my way to the feed bag. So I flung him from me and unfortunately he managed to find the large stairway and make his way down on his head. I was on my second helping when the police arrived. In fact if I did know his wife she had slipped my mind, and the now institutionalized husband has a wall eye, and for what? Was it worth it, that the last words falling from an over-rouged, collapsed beauty were about me? Bah!

As you see, I was adroit at dealing with mad women even from Florida shaking their fists at me. I swallowed the dregs of my drink and peered past Melanie at the empty waiter's post and sighed as I prepared myself for a granddaughter's scorn.

"She spoke very kindly of you, and wished that you two could have talked once more, as she always enjoyed your chats."

There was something terribly familiar about this young lady but I could not think what it was. I didn't want to appear wholly idiotic and ask who we were talking about, as it seemed as I was supposed to know all about it. I stared harder at my shoes. I had never noticed the workmanship around the toes, with the sewing and all. Bloody English, but they know what they are doing when it comes to cobbling. Oh, for God's sake.

"I am so sorry for your loss, but…." I started.

"Her name was Carolyn," she said.

"But I am not at all sure…"

"Carolyn A."

Explosion number two went off. The famous Mrs. A. was gone. A wellspring of memories bubbled up: Mrs. A kissing me all over, Mrs. A at the start of the whole thing. Mrs. A gone. I could not fathom it. I owed her so much, and I longed for the impossible, one more chat together with lashings of her tea and scones to go with it. Just when you want to wallow in your thoughts, the Battle of the Ardennes begins.

"And my mother is Grace A." That's it, I thought, I am for it now; get ready for the 400-metre dash to the car. Not a bit of it.

"My mother Grace died years ago of congestive heart failure in Scotland, so Nana raised me before she left for Florida. I work for a television network as a producer and am engaged to a lawyer."

She seemed oblivious to my discomfort and was in no hurry to finish her story. I had a terrible premonition of something dark coming my way and wished to vacate the premises, but could not as my limbs were frozen.

"I have been looking at you trying to imagine the affaire that you had…."

"Wait a minute, whatever your mother might have intimated… Ahhhhh…….This is outrageous, I am at my club after all," I sputtered.

"Not my mother, with Nana."

"Nana?" Surely Mrs. A wouldn't have said anything to her granddaughter? We are civilized, for God's sake!

"Your Nana said the I had a liaison with her?"

"Yes," she answered and smiled sweetly while waves of nausea surged about me below decks. Dash it all, if my current wife should get wind of this it could get tricky.

"I require a triple, my man, or I can't go on," I said, pushing the waiter towards the long bar by the stairs. The wretched girl now seemed to be catching a terrible case of the giggles. I found them in the worst possible taste and I wasted no time in telling her so.

"Errrrrr," I said strongly, but this only seemed to make matters worse. "Teeeeeeeeeeeeeheeeeee."

My heart went out to her fiancé. Even though he was a lawyer, they are still human up to a point. Beauty is always trumped by tee-hees. I returned to the battle but was relieved to note there seemed to be no road leading to her mother in the story.

"Now, your Nana said she and I were intimate more than 40 years ago?" That was a mistake, putting a time frame on it.

"You do remember it, I knew it, you couldn't have forgotten," she jumped on my tiny error like a conservative on a liberal. I sank further down into my chair. I could see the headline for the story by those scaly reporters from the Globe and Mail who would love to get their hands on a meaty subject such as this. Or the Toronto Star, where every single mother of colour is gracious and good while every old white man is an abomination. To think day after day I had spruced myself in the hope of receiving a smile from her dewy lips. Hopeless idiot!

"Nana thought you were marvellous, and was always talking about the great Robert Clarke." What an intelligent women this young woman was, can't think why I didn't spot that immediately.

"Do go on," I purred.

"Nana always said that Mum didn't deserve you and she and you had an understanding that you were both the great loves of each other's lives. I never knew my father, as I was born out of wedlock in 1967, when Mum went to Scotland." The final explosion went off. Could I possibly be her father? Ye gods and little frogs, this could not be happening.

"Mr. Clarke, you are drooling. Are you all right?" She was right, of course, for I had gone slack-jawed. She had said that any intimacy had been between her Nana and me, not between Grace and me. Perhaps Nana had chosen to leave it up to me to tell her. Or not. I took the plunge, as many brave Clarkes before me did.

"Did Mrs. A, that is to say your Nana, ever say who she thought your father was, just in passing, as it were?"

"Just that he was a wastrel and should be quickly forgotten."

A bit harsh, I thought, but under the circumstances, Mrs. A was smartly leaving no room for a rebuttal from her granddaughter. I was off the hook, except:

"Nana thought you might have something to say to me when we met. Do you?" Dratted woman, Nana. I pressed my temples and tried to think. It was obvious Nana thought I might confess all to this jumped-up fortune hunter, well, we Clarkes are made of firmer stuff.

"I think what your Nana was referring to was my old rule of never drinking too much on an empty stomach, very bad for your insides." She seemed inordinately disappointed with those pearls of wisdom. That's the trouble with the younger set these days, always looking for a bumper sticker philosophy instead of the fundamentals of life. How many of my late friends wished they had taken that advice. Right here at our club, my old school chum Knotsworthy Major, known as Laces, expired by the long bar. One night after a vigorous tennis match he refused to eat with the rest of us and straddled a bar stool instead. Whereupon after five large brandies, he blew his large bowel, told the head barman that he loved him and bled to death all over the memorial carpet. I was just about to tell Melanie about Laces when she said, "Nana thought it might be something more important than that."

More important than hearing about Laces? I suppose Mrs. A could have possibly meant telling Melanie that she might, repeat might, be my daughter. It was all so long ago and I have so many ungrateful children now. I rubbed my temples more. I tried again.

"Oh, and never marry a Muslim. It will end badly." Not bad under the circumstances. However Melanie was far from satisfied. She stood up and left.

Before you go off half-cocked, I want you to know that I did the right thing shortly thereafter. It was about the same time as the court ordered my DNA to be taken, but that was just a coincidence. Melanie joined our family and I had the great honour of giving her away to that dreadful lawyer chap a year later. The good news for me was that Mrs. A's side of the family had left Melanie very well off and in that spirit I spent her money lavishly on her wedding – only fair, after all.

A postscript: I just wish she hadn't been so keen to tell everyone about her Nana and me. My son claimed to be "freaked out" by the thought and my daughters offered no better, just a loud "yuck." My wife spent a fortune at Holt's as a revenge of sorts. This sin, if one must call it that, happened so many years ago, it is unfair to be seen now in the cold light of the present day. I remain innocent. Mrs. A and I only ever shared a bed once and it was crowded to say the least, but the fact that she remembered me so fondly is a wonderful gift from an extraordinary woman. Good night, Mrs. A.

All of which even makes me more determined that this book not see the light of day for one hundred years as previously discussed with my lawyers, the bastards.

Sitting here in my comfortable chair reminds me of going to England as a schoolboy to play cricket against as many public schools as we could in the three weeks allowed. It was a time of unequaled weather and pretty girls, and some damned fine cricket too. Near the end of the tour I was invited by a friend of my father's to visit his club for lunch.

The club turned out to be White's, which started at a former chocolate house in 1693 and was known as London's first club. Pope, Swift, Steel and Gray were some of its more celebrated members, plus Beau Brummell held court in the front window.

So on the Wednesday before our Friday flight back I presented myself in blazer, grey flannels, tie and highly polished oxfords to the porter at the front doors. I was allowed in to the front desk where I gave the name of the member I was to meet. The front-desk porter told me Sir James would be there shortly and would I mind waiting in the members' reading lounge, where tradition demands that no one speak. I picked up a Times from the foyer and entered the fabled lounge. How many great thoughts and plans for the Empire must have come from this room, as the giants of the past had shared a brandy or two, writing brief notes to each other. I was awash in the history that had taken place here, the redrawn maps of the world after a good lunch in the 1920s. The failed attempt to save Gordon at Khartoum in 1885, only to have Kitchener retake it in 1889. Eden fretting over the Suez or Macmillan worrying about Christine Keeler. All here.

I selected a beautiful spot in the bay window overlooking the street. The chair itself was a miracle of comfort; I imagined Disraeli relaxing in it, pondering the obstinacy of the widow Queen, Mrs. Brown. I opened the Times. Just then I noticed an ancient member making his way towards me. He seemed concerned about something, perhaps he had just come from a visit to his GP and had been told that was it for double martinis, If that was the case, I was sorry for him, for I had been lucky enough to have had my first earlier that trip. I had a lifetime to look forward to them, and I have doggedly applied myself in that area of endeavor.

As I waited for the old chap to arrive at the bay window, I noticed quite a few of the other members were staring in our direction so I spread a winning smile about the place. While normally people would return my smile, a chill seemed to run through the august room. The old member gave me a rheumy goggle, then leaned forward and actually went,

"Grrrrrrrrrrrrrrrrrr," but very quietly.

The veins on his great bald dome became three-dimensional and he seemed to be in some sort of extremis. I nodded kindly and put my paper up to my face in an attempt to read something rather than witness a stroke. Two gnarled hands gripped the top of my paper and tried to wrest it from me, which I naturally attempted to prevent, with the obvious result that the Times was rent apart.

The ancient member began to pant, and tried to sit on me as if he was in Aden or somewhere one does that to the natives. The mouths of the rest of the crowd were working silently but intently. I shoved the club member off me, perhaps a little too vigorously, as he was much lighter than I thought. He soared through the air and bounced off a Queen Victoria settee, coming to rest beside the large Chinese vase now shaking dangerously above the disoriented ruin.

A flunky sprinted from the far side of the room after dropping his drink order onto the 300-year-old Persian rug and saved the vase with only seconds to spare. I applauded, thinking if Campbell minimus had moved that quickly in our game a fortnight ago against Winchester we might have won the day. At the sound of my appreciative applause everybody in the lounge stood up, threw their papers to the ground and moved as a herd out the double doors to the adjoining library.

A very pale porter made his way towards me, writing something madly on his pad, which he thrust into my face. It read, "You are sitting in Lord Duncan's chair. He is our oldest member. Please remove yourself immediately." The aged Lord

Duncan could be seen trying to right himself over by the vase. Someone could have given me a hint that the bugle boy from the Crimean War wanted his chair back. How was I to know?

When I reached the foyer I was accosted by many of the old gentlemen who had left the lounge in such a rush earlier, one of them saying, "The last noise made in the lounge was when Lord North farted on being told of the Boston Tea Party in 1773, and you had the temerity to clap your hands. Outrageous."

Just then Sir James took me by the arm into lunch. It was a strained meal, as Sir James thought his name had taken a hit because of my actions, something that was only made worse by my insistence on having ice in my gin and tonic.

"Might I ask if you are a Mohawk, or of some other tribe?" he inquired sarcastically. All because he said it wasn't done to have ice in your drink in England. I said nothing until he had led me to the door after a mediocre lunch. He took my hand and tried to squeeze the hell out of it to teach me a lesson. I took his little finger as we had been taught in Major Iggulden's self-defense lessons at Ridley, and bent it far back against his hand, which brought him abruptly to his knees in the street outside the club. Still holding his throbbing digit I put my mouth close to his ear and whispered, "Fuck off, you effete English prick." I had a new and cheerful stride as I made my way up to Piccadilly and back to the hotel.

CHAPTER 13

(This chapter was found by the cleaning staff at Robert's beloved club, but exactly where is not clear. We have no comment except it appears to be genuine Robert. ED)

So now at my club I push away anyone I find at my chair, and it works a treat. I must now return to my schooling as this memoir would not be fully realized without a few words on my days at Ridley College. I finished Crescent in the upper seventh form. The school actually went to the upper eighth form, but my father felt I should start at Ridley a year early so as to do a full two years in the Lower School. He knew if I did Eight and Nine, I might make duty boy by Nine, which was the equivalent of an upper school prefect. It was all so complicated and strange, but that was what all-boys boarding schools were like in the 1950s.

The school is in the town of St. Catharines. If you know Toronto, you will also know that when you drive on the Queen Elizabeth highway to Niagara Falls, you pass the industrial town of St. Catharines, deep in the heart of Ontario's wine district. I sat dejected in Father's MK 9 Jaguar, dreading this large and frightening school as the miles flew by. I had been there several times before as I had to sit for the entrance exams and Father had taken me there for the Gym Night, as well as sundry cricket games.

Ridley was not the little, now-friendly school of my past, Crescent. This was 400 boys spread over a vast acreage, with the most menacing masters known to man. There had always been a Clarke at Ridley and it was at least interesting to see my great ancestors scattered across the Sport Wall on the way to the chapel. In those long-ago photos from the 1880s and '90s, the athletes lounged on the lawn in haphazard groups, appearing indifferent to their sport or the photographer, much at odds from the photos of today with everyone sitting straight up and on risers. I preferred the old way.

The only incident of note on the trip to my new school outside of my trepidation was that Father hit a farmer's dog near Vineland. I took this as a bad sign, but not Father, who handed the stunned farmer ten dollars. "Oh, no, my boy, this simply removes the bad from the future. You wait and see, Robert, it will be happy days from now on."

I was not convinced. Ridley had a reputation for incorrigibles. Children who had run amok were sent there, generally for harsh discipline such as the cane. At Crescent we were beaten from sun-up to sundown, but not with a cane, as was used at Ridley with, we had heard, great abandon. Since I was always in trouble, I felt it wouldn't be long before I felt the cane's sting.

We passed beneath the imposing gates of the school right on time, for Father was a stickler for punctuality, and pulled up in front of the Lower School entrance. The greatest teacher of cricket I would ever know stood scrutinizing me as I disembarked.

"Does this boy purport to play cricket, sir?" barked the master.

"He does!" shouted my father just as aggressively, as I shrank to half of my height.

"My name is Burns and the boy's name is… " said Mr. Burns loudly.

"He is Robert Clarke and I am Mr. Clarke," said Father. He was not going to have a two-bit teacher talk to him like that.

"Clarke? Well, my boy, I have been waiting for you," Mr. Burns said. "Mr. Noonan from your former school asked me to watch for you, as he claimed that you were quite a cricketer."

Dear old Mr. Noonan had smoothed my way into the next school. Unfortunately cricket season didn't start for six months. Nevertheless I had been introduced to Mr. Burns under the best possible circumstances. The boys in the lower school called him "Frog" Burns, and indeed he was an exact replica of a frog. He had a wide, thin-lipped mouth with eyes that seemed to rotate at will. He was English, of course, and mad, but a character and a great deal of fun. He had broken every blood vessel in his face so that he looked not unlike someone who has been hit with tomato soup while sitting in a convertible going at some speed.

Frog had flown two-seater Mosquito bombers, which were made of plywood, during the war. So to keep from being incinerated he would throw them into vertical dives to avoid the ack-ack and present a smaller target. He pushed those little planes far beyond their specs with the steepness of those dives and would often return to base with some of the veins in his face gone and blood seeping from the corners of his eyes. When Burns became angry during geography class, his face took on a hue that could have guided ships at sea.

I said goodbye to my father, who appeared proud that I was entering the school as so many in our family had before me, and I watched as his white Jag disappeared into the distance. An older boy from the upper ninth grade was assigned to show me the way to my dorm, but he refused to help with my trunk and bags. I hated him instantly and began to feel more comfortable as it dawned on me that I had been at boarding school for most of the five years at Crescent and I was not yet twelve. I knew this game and was good at it.

There was no fear in my heart, not after appearing at the age of eight to be strapped by old Mr. Williams. I suddenly saw that those around me were more terrified and didn't know what to expect, while I was an old hand at this and understood what was coming.

The older boy was a fool called Chatsworth who was clearly a teacher's pet and was up for the duty boy position, hence his helping with new boys like me. I knew his kind. I surmised that I was much stronger than he was.

"Pick up the trunk, Chatsworth," I commanded, which he did immediately. I liked this place already.

We arrived at my dorm on the second floor of the Lower School, which was called Tecumseh, named for the greatest Canadian Indian general and one of the finest anywhere. He fought for Canada against the Americans in the War of 1812, and was lethal by all accounts, taking many battles, including Detroit with Brock. Because of an incompetent British general, Tecumseh was killed at the Thames in 1813. In typical Canadian fashion there is little acknowledgement of this great warrior in the country he fought for, but his enemies admired and respected him. So in the middle of Washington you will find a truly beautiful and imposing sculpture of OUR fallen hero. Strange.

Anyway I followed that idiot Chatsworth into my new home and looked around. There are a few things you must understand about living in a fifteen-person dorm. One never takes the KV bed, the one closest to the door, because you will be the first seen by the approaching master, or you will be beaten by your dorm-mates for not giving adequate warning of said master's imminent arrival, so you can't win. The term KV comes from the Latin term "beware" and don't ask me what the actual words are, for it has been more than fifty years since this happened. Look them up yourself, lazy bastards.

I feel quite rowdy thinking of those physical days when might was right. Chatsworth tried to put my trunk by the KV bed and for that I kicked him hard in the shin and he hopped out of the dorm truly in fear of me. I looked to the rear of Tecumseh dorm for the bed furthest from the door, and there it was with a little fat kid sitting forlornly with a tin of biscuits held firmly in his lap. Remember this is Lord of the Flies kind of stuff, and let us not forget my introduction to dorm-life at the age of seven at my previous school. I sauntered to the back of the dorm and looked down at the frightened boy.

"I am afraid this is my bed, now move along, there's a good lad." I was very pleasant, but I wanted the bed and he didn't have a clue how valuable it was strategically Unfortunately sometimes even out of shape new boys show inappropriate bravery.

"Go away, it's mine," he said. It turned out later Lester was from Rochester, N.Y., and had to be dragged bodily across the border to attend the school his father did. Here was the problem. The bed was at the end of a row of seven beds, directly in line with the KV bed but much further removed from the door, so that you could see everything the KV bed did but have time to adjust before the duty master was on us.

Those factors were key for a carefree year, I knew from my years in the third-floor dorms at Crescent, so I was not going to let this little boy determine my fate in the Tecumseh dorm. It didn't take much in the end, just a short, sharp punch to his right eye. He howled as I gathered his things and placed them far away on the KV bed by the door. What one has to learn early at a boys' school is that the cavalry isn't coming, that no one is going to save little Jimmy or Johnny, no, they just go on being beaten till they learn to survive. They are alone, most for the first time in their lives, and they were miserable, just as Lester was miserable. They had to understand that their mother and father had put them in a place where the institutional punishment is the strap or the cane, they knew that and were paying a lot of money for you to be flogged at anytime. QED.

The sobbing was not off-putting. I had heard it many times before; often it had been me. It was a good lesson for Lester to get out of the way early. A black eye was a small price to pay.

The dorm began to fill up but I only had to fight two other boys for the right to call the bed mine; if this had been my old dorm there would have been a dozen. While both of them had gone to private school they had not boarded and so not learned to fight dirty. The first came at me in the classic boxing style, fists up around his face and his elbows held close together. Mr. Noonan had always insisted that you should let the other chap make the first move and if his swing missed he would be off balance and the world was yours. Clifford, a tall boy from Montreal, tried to put me out on the first swing, I ducked and did as Mr. Noonan had done in hundreds of fights. I dropped to my knees and grabbed Clifford's balls. First I twisted them harshly to get his attention and by his wild dancing movements I felt I had. As per Mr. N's instructions, I began to crush them. That brought Clifford down for a short, pleading chat. Not normally a lip reader I could still make out that Clifford didn't think I was playing by the eighth Marquis of Queensbury rules. I squeezed harder, and Clifford's eyes rolled back in his head. He did, however, indicate that his previous position had been revised and that the bed by the communal washrooms would do nicely.

The next kid, Smith, was broad of beam with hair all over his back. Once again Mr. Noonan swam into view and I waited until he had his strong arms around my ribcage and had begun to squeeze. First I struck the bridge of his nose with my forehead, which produced an immediate and very red gusher. Smith moaned in pain, but stupidly hung on, and since I couldn't tell where his nose was any more due to the abundance of blood, I went to plan B. I took both of my hands and brought them back behind my head. I am sure Smith knew what was coming but not unlike his early simian ancestors his mind was not quick. I brought my palms together in a frightening move that slapped both of his ears at the same time. That was it; the so-called fight was over. Smith ran in small circles dribbling and anxious for sympathy. There was none forthcoming. He claimed for years after that he could hear an obscure radio station in Waco, Texas, with little static.

I now possessed the bed I had wanted in the first place and I set about making friends as one needed allies for the coming term. My first friend at Ridley was Blanchard, I am not sure I ever knew his first name, just Blanchard. There was a certain coolness of style about him, a together sort of individual. Adequate at sports, an indifferent student, but highly amusing — he was the Tecumseh clown. There was something else about him that gave the rest of us pause. He had whacked off before. At our age this function was almost apocryphal. We thought of it as a distant and disgusting rumour, and yet before us stood someone who could bear witness to it. We were all, of course, aware of the constant boners that we had to endure, and that their use was to somehow insert it into women, but we never had actually discussed the term sperm, or as Blanchard referred to it, jiz. Blanchard watched us scratch, at least metaphorically, our collective heads, no doubt enjoying the new-found power he had. Morgan (no relation to my friend at Crescent), a boy of a painfully pedantic outlook, said finally, "Show us."

This happened about the third week of school so that the dorm was beginning to coalesce into a sort of rudimentary society. Burnside, Blanchard and I were at the top of the heap, with Lester bringing up the rear. Everyone else was a sort of villager who would go with the strongest element.

"For fifty cents each, Blanchard will whack off," I said suddenly. My money was all spent for the month, and it went unsaid that Blanchard and I would split the swag. Everyone started speaking at once, as this was an enormous amount of money. Hilyard said if they did agree then Blanchard must be completely naked, for there could be no suspicion of a foreign liquid such as Resdan being substituted for the real stuff as no one had ever seen the real stuff and certainly no one was going to touch it. There was a suggestion that we force Lester to taste it to see what it was, but just at that moment Lester was seen breaking the 50 yard dash record on his way down the stairs, and was therefore no longer in the equation.

Blanchard and I met to discuss terms in the bathroom and surprisingly he had no objection to being stripped. So I returned to the dorm to address the waiting troops. I laid out the rules as follows:

1. Blanchard would be stripped but gently as we didn't want to lose the mood.
2. Blanchard would be allowed his privacy until the moment of truth at which point we would be called to witness the exhibition.
3. Blanchard would be allowed to take the National Geographic magazine with him, opened at the article, "East African Pygmies in all their glory."

This was agreed to, although Higgens kept saying we were all headed for hell. Several of the villagers felt that they were already in hell, but there are always whiners amongst any group. The negotiations completed, Morgan stripped Blanchard, a little roughly, I thought, but Blanchard said nothing and proceeded royally to the dorm kibo, shutting the door behind him. We stood in groups waiting expectantly, not knowing exactly what was in store, only that it might be a momentous occasion.

Silence ensued and the villagers became restless about their money, which I held in my blazer pockets. I fixed them with one of my "hungry panther staring at the tethered goat" looks, which brought most of them into line, except Morgan, who always seemed ready to give a Tom Paine-style speech about freedom and other such crap, which should never be allowed to take hold in a boys dorm. I judged that this might unnerve the others again, so I punched him hard on his upper arm. Then we heard a little groan from the closed door and everyone started shushing the others. I laid into them, slapping heads and ear-holes with great abandon, like Blackbeard must have had to do occasionally while sitting off Port Royal. All fell silent again, then a slightly louder noise, then silence again. Perhaps the Pygmies were not enough, although there was one picture on page 341 of four of the more fetching Pygmy women. There came another little groan, then another with much slapping of flesh and more noises.

This was new to even the most sophisticated of us, including Burnside, who once had tea with the Queen at the behest of his diplomat father. We sat waiting for we knew not what. Soon it became clear that the engine had left the station, for Blanchard began to bellow so loudly that lovely Gerta from the sewing and laundry room adjacent to our dorm door flew down to see what was the matter.

"Vas is tha?" she said.

"It's some boy missing his mother, Gerda," said Hilyard, thinking fast, but he was shortly undone by an interjection from Blanchard.

"They are SO beautiful and small, oh my GOD!"

"That no sound like boy missing mother, that sound like boy being dirty," Gerda said.

"Oh my Christ, this is it. OOOOOOOOOOO." said Blanchard. Gerda rushed to the washroom door and flung it open at the same time as Blanchard was staggering out of his stall, still urging his engorged member for the show and tell. He promptly deposited 100 cc onto the starched uniform of Gerda, who had recently arrived from a war zone.

"Ahhhh, a Russian who vants to rape!" screamed Gerda, who then very accurately deposited the end of her foot into the surprised groin of Blanchard. The villagers and I started running for our lives as we knew this incident would bring about a Royal Commission of some sort, leading soon thereafter to a drumhead trial or at least strappings all round for all those caught in the vicinity.

When Blanchard later came out of the infirmary with hugely swollen testes he had lost any sense of humour, so I stood him to one of his favourite treats, Turkish Delight from the Tuck Shop. As he munched and waddled with me out to the soccer field he said he had completed his end of the bargain, so where was his share of the money? I pointed out that while there was some circumstantial evidence in the screams from Gerda and the way she held the front of her dress, technically our group had seen no visual proof and were asking for the return of their money. He said that was because we had vacated the judges' platform before he was finished, so the tie should go to him, the participant. In the end he and I split the money. It caused a bit of a stink with the others but who could they take their case to?

As for the expected punishment, luckily Gerda could not make herself understood to the Headmaster, or even the other women in the sewing room. The most anyone could make out was something about "Blanchard giving life," so the matter was dropped.

The married and unmarried masters at the school lived in vastly different quarters. The married masters' quarters were situated at both ends of the school and consisted of three bedrooms, a formal dining and living room, a splendid kitchen and very useable back gardens. The bachelor quarters, on the other hand, had two rooms, a sitting room and a bedroom, and no kitchen with just a miserable bathroom to round it off. The bachelor masters seemed to come and go on a yearly basis. They earned about $1,500 a year, but with free room and board as they ate with us in the large dining room, it wasn't really a bad deal in the 1950s. The money kept them in cigarettes and booze, plus enough left over to run a tiny car of some kind.

One of the bachelor masters was Mr. Tracy, whose small apartment was at the end of the hallway between the two dorms, the other dorm named Brant after the great Iroquois chief Joseph Brant. Mr. Tracy was a psychological train-wreck who was vicious to us at every opportunity. He used to beat me in the masters' study, where these punishments took place, at three in the morning, having decided before lights-out who would suffer that night, and he didn't like me at all. This stemmed from an earlier occasion when Mr. Tracy had invited me to his rooms as he turned off the lights in the second-floor dorms. The invitation was not unusual, for as boys we were always hungry, and Sir would offer sausages late at night done on his coal fireplace.

While the school fed us enormous amounts three times a day, I don't know how many of you could eat a full tongue that still looked like a cow's tongue when it was served, torn from its moorings in a cow's mouth, as the table master sliced through the obvious taste buds. They were disgusting. Several boys were ill and later flogged under the heading of "cheek in the Memorial Dining Room." The American kids tried to get us to eat ketchup on bread but that was too frightful for even my sensibilities. There were many other meals that were too appalling to do more than pick at, a soup, for instance, served in huge cauldrons with what appeared to be fish heads floating around, oddly several looked like an uncle of mine. The English masters, though, seemed to eat anything after war rationing they had endured back home.

If you still had a little money, there was the Tuck Shop, which opened twice a day for thirty minutes, exactly thirty minutes and no more. But if you were out of money or they closed the Tuck Shop before the retired master who augmented his pension with the profits from the shop could serve you, then you would hope for an invitation from Mr. Tracy.

There was a steep downside to these nocturnal visits: Mr. Tracy's need for little boys. To give him his due he never hurt any of us physically but it was revolting nevertheless. Many older boys were buggered senseless by the upper school prefects, but rarely down in the lower school, but we still had Mr. Tracy. After the official lights out, you would put on your dressing gown and slippers, then traverse the hallway to Mr. Tracy's room, whose door was slightly ajar. The room would be warm and cozy with the master already in bed and fully naked. With a "come hither" grin, he would indicate the long fork with several sausages on a plate beside the fireplace.

"But first your master needs a hug," he would say huskily. We hated that part as we wanted the food first, but what could one do? So I went over to his bed and let him hug me. To many of these Englishmen deodorant was an unknown term as was a nightly bath, and I will remember his drunken breath till the day I die. The stench almost put me off what I was there for, but the four nearby sausages beckoned to me as the serpent to Eve. He released me and I shot over to the fireplace, pronging the first of the sausages as I went. The fire was marvelous and the sausage was cooked in no time. I happened to glance out of the window, which looked back at my dorm, and was touched to see several of my friends staring back with worried looks on their faces. I waved them off in a carefree fashion and started the second as I gorged on the first. Mr. Tracy was getting impatient.

"Come over here, boy, the food will wait," he said. Franklin, a villager, had warned us that once you returned to his side, that would be it for the food, for he had only managed to eat one. I started cooking the third and had one and a half in my mouth.

"Don't be a fool, boy, you can't possibly eat them all, COME HERE," Mr. Tracy said. Things were heating up for me, as I cooked the fourth and last one while secreting the third in my dressing gown.

"Almost done, sir, won't be moment, sir," I said through a mouthful of sausage.

"I am not asking you, Clarke, I am telling you, now COME HERE OR YOU WILL BE THE SORRIER FOR IT."

I stood up with my almost cooked sausage and took off my dressing gown and put it by the door. I knew the drill. I would lie down on his small bed with my back to Mr. Tracy, at which point he would put one unwashed arm around me and then do something unspeakable to himself and that would be it, I could leave.

"Stay still, boy," he whispered as he fussed with himself and pulled me to him. Then the bed started to shake in short bursts with him saying disgusting things into my ear. I did not yet pretend to be an expert on things such as climaxes (no offense, Matron), so I worked on the time element, and when after a few minutes I thought that I had completed the contract, I broke away and made for the door. Apparently Mr. Tracy was not finished, for he let out a cry of a wounded animal while pawing at the air to bring me back. For me it was over and I headed out into the hallway with my purloined sausage, tremendously impressed with myself. I had beaten the system, I thought.

How stupid I was, for there is no escape, as I well knew. A few minutes later I felt the side of my bed decline as Mr. Tracy sat down. He took my ear and wordlessly almost tore it off, then returned to his rooms. I knew I had made a terrible enemy for the rest of the school year.

In spite of the sword of Damocles hanging over me I had a wonderful time that first year at Ridley. I thought we had a great deal of sports at Crescent, but it was nothing compared to this place. We talked about the different teams from dawn to dusk, as in who would make the third Eleven or the second soccer team, not to mention diving, swimming, football, hockey, cricket, rugby, fencing, cross-country Harriers, squash, tennis, gym, shooting, and cadets, plus the glee club and debating teams for the sports-challenged. It was a fabulous place to grow up.

The school itself had been founded in 1889, the year of Hitler's birth, as we loved reminding our parents, by the Anglican Church as a school that turned out men who were fit both physically and spiritually. It was named after Bishop Ridley, the weakest of the three bishops burned by Bloody Mary upon her succession to the English throne. Henry the Eighth's son Edward was weak physically and only ruled for six years before expiring. Latimer and Ridley were taken to the stake in Oxford and burned alive. Thomas Cranmer joined them in the fire a few months later in 1556. The motto of the school was Terrar Dom Prosim or "May I be consumed in service." We preferred the schoolboy motto "Tear down our prison." At this school we wore grey flannels, a school tie and a black blazer with orange trim, along with the ubiquitous black oxfords. We were treated more as adults than at Crescent.

My favourite teacher was Mr. Osler, a failed Shakespearean actor with the voice of God. It came as a low rumble, then spread like the Mongols sweeping across Asia Minor, ending in a thunderclap. He could make "class dismissed" sound biblical.

I had the great honour of spending hours in the small but crammed library in his bachelor quarters listening to him read passages from his favourite authors: Scott, Kipling, Tennyson and Dickens. The spoken word and the modulated tone of a trained actor blessed me with a love of English that I am grateful for every day of my life, and we boys became the products of men such as Mr. Osler. For every Mr. Tracy there were half a dozen great educators standing in the wings. I enjoyed everything about that first year, even the beatings, almost.

Christopher Dalton

I must pause as a thirst has taken root in my soul and only the silver liquid of my beloved martini will allow me to endure these schoolboy memories and carry on.

Blanchard had many things to teach us, bless him, for he was by far the worldliest of our bunch.

"Clarke, are you awake?" he whispered from the next bed to mine.

"Yes," instantly alert to danger.

"Do you know what a circle jerk is?" I didn't have a clue. "Tomorrow after math I'll show you." I went back to sleep knowing it would be something dark.

By this time, most of us had achieved a new and higher level of manhood thanks to Blanchard in that we had experienced the petite mort, so to speak. An offshoot (it's the martinis, I'm afraid) was that we were developing bigger muscles in our right arms from constant use, for not unlike gambling, it is madly addictive. Every night after lights out page 341, long ago ripped from the National Geographic with our friends the Pygmies on it, would be passed around. The physics of the situation demanded that the flashlight was held in one's mouth while the head and one arm formed a tent, leaving the right arm to do its duty.

All went smoothly until Morgan's aim was off one night and he hit the Pygmy third from the right. In his embarrassment he folded the precious page in two, fusing with his DNA the two folds forever. He denied it, of course, just before we beat him, but the poor sod to his left who was waiting for the page sobbed with bitterness. I had no need for the Pygmies as all I had to do was cast my mind back to Molly in the sub-basement at Crescent for I now understood what all of her bits and bobs were for. But a circle jerk?

There were five of us who gathered in the dorm after math. Blanchard joined us, late as always, but waving a new magazine above his head.

"I got the latest Stag mag from the masters' study, " he said triumphantly. We blanched. Burnside spoke for us all.

"They, they, they wiiiiiiiiiiii… will go mad, Blanchard."

But Blanchard laughed that. "Oh yeah? Who will they tell, boys?" Brilliant! Well up to a point, because we knew things wouldn't rest there, but Blanchard was eager to return to the purpose of the meeting.

"OK, everyone take off your clothes." We walked around nude in the locker rooms and of course swam naked in the upper school pool, so we did as we were bidden. Blanchard tore a few of the pages out of the stolen magazine and placed them so as we formed the circle everyone would be able to view one or more of the smutty photos. Stag was famous for having women of tremendous sized breasts, always looking surprised at being photographed. There would be a small tree or a fake background of some sort so that it wouldn't look like the tiny studio in Burbank that it was.

Now we got to the actual rules of the circle jerk. "Lie in a circle and take the pecker of the chap to your right in your hand and whack him off — get it?" Blanchard said. Seemed simple enough, take the boy to your right and pull till ….

"Wait a minute, we have learned how to do this ourselves," I complained. "Why do we need somebody to do it for us?" Several boys nodded their heads vigorously.

"Because, you idiot, it will feel different and hence more exciting!" There was unassailable logic in that, as one did get a little used to the same thing six or seven times a day. The other day Mr. Nind, the master on duty, caught Law, a large and stupid boy, playing madly with himself in the bath room, which consisted of four baths and nothing else. Mr. Nind went berserk as Law was doing it in front of some Lower Sixth boys who were completely befuddled by what he was trying to achieve. Mr. Nind took the well-lit and large pipe from his mouth and, using the stem, hit Law extremely hard on the top of his head with the bowl of the pipe. The result was an explosion of sparks. Flaming tobacco filled the bath room and four boys submerged, three of them to escape the furnace-like atmosphere and the other because he was concussed. Mr. Nind reached a tweedy arm into Law's bath to pull him above the water level and screamed, "You are an animal, Law, an animal!" Then he released Law, who had missed the chairman's remarks altogether and sank back to his underwater kingdom.

In other words, masturbation was as prevalent as breathing in the lower school, at least in our minds. None of us in the circle that day was homosexual and as far as I know no one became one. We were discovering our bodies at what is normally a difficult time for young men. However here there were only young men, so you could discover yourself among equals. As disgusting as it might sound, this is how it was and most of us turned out all right in the end.

Back to the dorm. We formed our circle and tentatively took the boy's member to our right into our hands. To say that was an odd feeling was a staggering understatement. Then Blanchard said, "OK, look at the pictures and start to do it." In retrospect, this is funny, because Blanchard now owns a DO-IT renovation store in Alberta somewhere, which as you know is a DIY store. Anyway we all began rubbing and stroking and the complaints started almost immediately.

"Morgan is hurting my knob," and "It's too fast, slow down," and "No fair, Clifford is a lefty, he can't do it properly." Blanchard stood up quickly, clipped Clifford on the ear and told him to smarten up, lefty or not. Everything was solved in those days by a slap or two. Clifford soldiered on, until he said, "My arm is getting sore," but Morgan wasn't having any of that.

"Don't stop, you bastard," he said wildly.

"Arm…sore," proclaimed Clifford, but he could hardly move because the boy on his left was having some effect on him. Morgan shot off two full bed lengths, upon which Burnside couldn't stop giggling, which began to play havoc with our collective imagination. I had to concentrate on my pic of Mary-Louise, who, it said, wanted to help the poor and liked to be without clothes when outdoors. She had the usual "caught unawares," but her incredibly large breasts made her easy to focus on, so I was able to complete my mission and not look foolish.

The problem was Morgan, Blanchard and I were finished, yet we were required to help the other two over their personal hurdles. Morgan and I became positively desultory. In fact now that we were finished the situation struck us as disgusting and we stopped altogether. The other two shouted in outrage and were forced to retire to the dorm washroom with their photographs. When everyone had crossed home plate, Blanchard gathered up the evidence of the purloined magazine and deposited it under the mattress of Lester. That night two red-faced and slightly drunken masters arrived at our dorm about one in the morning, flipping on the lights and turning over our beds. Lester's treasure trove was found within minutes, causing Lester to throw himself at the Latin master, cling to his leg while singing hymns and babbling about injustice. He was torn from the leg and led away by the scruff of his neck to be thrashed.

Our education on all fronts carried on. My contribution other than my "previous boarder" wisdom was to teach my dorm mates the toothpaste cannon. This entailed buying a giant-sized tube of Gleam toothpaste at the Tuck Shop, which was one of the few things you could charge to your parents' tab (Gleam was the only toothpaste available). We would then run back to Tecumseh, open the windows and watch the other dorm across the quadrangle. The one opposite ours was called Laurier after the great Canadian PM, whose residents that year did not play sports well and seemed to populate the debating and glee clubs. When one of the boys from Laurier would open a window, we were ready.

The trick was to place the giant toothpaste tube slightly over the half-way mark on the window sill and then bring our window down hard. If done correctly, the result would be a incredible stream of toothpaste shooting across the quad, two stories up and straight through a window of Laurier, hitting with some force an unsuspecting dimwit.

It was almost the perfect crime. In fact, Mr. Muggeridge witnessed it at two in the morning and put it down to having consumed a bad batch of the headmaster's sherry.

Of course we ultimately got caught and strapped for our trouble, because if the tube was balanced dead centre on the sill rather than slightly closer to Laurier, both ends would blow, causing a fierce toothpaste explosion and covering the cannon crew with evidence.

One afternoon when I was at swimming, Morgan and few of the villagers tried to emulate the process and created a massive backfire, giving proof to the hitherto unbelievable accusations from Laurier dorm.

When I returned to the dorm, Mr. Tracy and the headmaster were eyeballing the white and sticky window and its environs. Mass strappings took place that night, including the once again wholly innocent Lester, who was turning into a bit of a case due to the unfairness meted out upon him. We beat Morgan, of course, who denied any involvement but he had been informed on by a bitter delegation of villagers.

Mr. Tracy was becoming a thorn in our sides. He now skulked around the dorm in a highly suspicious mood, which to us was unfair. He was always fishing, which is not cricket, really. The rules of combat were that we had to do something first and then he could come looking, not the other way around. But he was continuously going through the private boxes that sat under our beds, or rummaging through our lockers, throwing the contents on the floor afterwards.

Burnside came up with a brilliant plan, which I put down to my influence. There were two entrances to the quad, both facing the upper school, with the inside of the quad being a dead end of classrooms. The entrances had been designed long before cars had been thought of, and so were only suitable for three boys abreast with no vehicular traffic possible. Burnside had calculated that Mr. Tracy's Austin Zephyr weighed about 900 pounds, which divided by fifteen boys, even allowing for Lester, would be sixty pounds per boy to lift. On Saturday nights it was Mr. Tracy's habit to visit downtown St. Catharines, as he was free from duty after the early dinner at six. From the dinner hour on, our time was our own, however Mr. Tracy visited our dorm once more before leaving for town.

"Well, you dreadful human monsters, as your dorm was the worst again this week, you will forfeit your half day on Wednesday and stay in these sty-like quarters to contemplate your lack of cleanliness."

When he finished, he showed us his rotten teeth like an enraged baboon and was gone. Strangely, it was Lester who showed anger at this. The school week consisted of full days Monday, Tuesday, Thursday and Friday, with half days Wednesday and Saturday. On those half days, we attended class in the mornings and were allowed to go downtown after our sports commitments, so that the streets of St. Catharines teemed with boys from the upper and lower schools. As it happened, Lester was to give a recital at St. Thomas church in town on Wednesday, for he was a first-class organist. This was because of visit by a virtuoso, he and others from the Niagara vicinity had been asked to play at the church. Lester snapped. He pulled a knife stolen from the dining room and started down the hall to carve his name in Mr. Tracy's backside, and several of us had to calm him by sitting on his chest while promising him revenge.

Then we waited for the return of Mr. Tracy. At three-thirty in the morning Lester shook my shoulder to let me know he was back and together we woke the others. We watched silently watched as he staggered up the stairs to his rooms, sporting a black eye, with the collar of his one suit completely missing. The sounds coming from his tiny washroom indicated he was being violently ill. We waited by his door as he cried, "Oh, God, never again, I am so ashamed….Forgive me, God, I am weak, so weak." After one more purge, he collapsed on his bed and started snoring immediately.

We gave the all-clear to the rest of the dorm and headed for the outside doors. We found his little car half-parked in the garden beside the entrance to the quad with the doors unlocked. This was not surprising as no one in those days locked anything. Blanchard put the car in neutral as the rest of us rolled it so the hood was pointing into the quad. Burnside had been in charge of bringing the blankets, which we spread out on one side of the car, and on a signal, we took up positions on the opposite side of the car from the blankets. On a very quiet count of three, we turned the car on its side onto the blankets.

Each boy was given a position around the car; some would be more arduous than others. For instance, two boys would push up and lift, holding the tires that were already facing them, so their lift wasn't very far. Others had to squat and lift from the gravel driveway all the way up to our shoulder height with no grips for our hands. We almost dropped the car on the first try, but by the third attempt we had got the hang of it and walked magnificently into the quad carrying Mr. Tracy's car in a sideways position.

Burnside picked a spot right in the middle, and we put the car down, righting it as we went. We could not believe what we had done and hugged each other in glee, although Lester wanted to cut him anyway. The next morning, although tired, we manned the windows in expectation. The first sign of something extraordinary was Mr. Tracy being woken by another master.

"James!" said Mr. Cover. Nothing came from Mr. Tracy's room. "James, for God's sake, man, your car is in the quad."

"What," said Mr. Tracy groggily, for he had no duty calls till the afternoon and found this intrusion unexpected at best. Finally the door opened and Mr. Cover went in. A few seconds later there were Mr. Tracy and Mr. Cover looking out of the window at the car in the quad. We could see although not hear Mr. Tracy say to his friend, "But that's impossible."

Mr. Tracy quickly dressed and raced down the stairs to the quad. We imagined what was going through his head as he ran. "I guess in my drunkenness I inadvertently parked it in the quad, but how is that possible, it shouldn't fit. Oh God, I must get that thing out of there before the Head finds out, as he never liked me much anyway. I think he may be a little suspicious of my academic qualifications and rightly so as I never really attended Cambridge, much less graduated with honours .... Got to fix this quick." Or something like that.

Every window that looked down upon the quad was jammed with boys, as Romans looking at an optimistic Christian before the poor chap realizes he is the first course on the menu. There was, however, no pity in the eyes of the boys from the lower school that glorious Sunday morning.

Mr. Tracy had arrived at the quad and was looking from the stone entrance to his car and back again as if measuring sizes and shapes. The boys began to lo like cattle at an abattoir, louder and louder, with Mr. Tracy hopping around with a sickly smile on his face trying to shush them. It was a rare thing that boys see justice done and this was to be savoured. The din became louder as Mr. Tracy's look changed to rage, made worse by the sight of Lester drawing a knife across his throat as a sign to the master that he was dead.

Mr. Tracy was spitting at the windows in fury when the head and several masters came running into the quad, which caused Mr. Tracy to jump into his car and start the engine. Perhaps he thought if he had got in last night, then he would get out this morning. He gunned his car towards the nearest entrance while waving nonchalantly at the headmaster as he shot past him. I have been told the Halifax Harbour explosion during the first World War was the loudest noise ever heard, but those of us there that morning might disagree as metal met stone at high speed.

Mr. Tracy almost made it through, but physics will not allow its firm and fair laws to be breached. The little Austin sat snugly in the arms of the stone archway, with Mr. Tracy continuing to press the accelerator to the floor. The cacophony almost ruptured our eardrums and even the deaf teacher Mr. Henning arrived to see what nuclear device had been unleashed. The boys of the lower school began to cheer wildly, waving scarves and such as if the school had claimed a great victory.

Then it was the headmaster's turn to try to keep order in the face of heavy odds, which became even heavier as we watched Mr. Tracy attempt to open his door. He was securely wedged in what seemed a slightly thinner car. We laughed and cheered as even the head gave up and walked sadly away. Mr. Tracy began screaming and we bayed back at him through the windows, pure joy.

It took hours to get the car loose. Mr. Tracy had pushed out the front window with his feet and was no longer in it when the two tow trucks pulled the wreckage through the quad entrance. Mr. Tracy went at first to find Lester, for he had been doing his knife and throat act through the car window as if baiting a bear. We surrounded Lester and said nothing, as Mr. Tracy burned bright, then ran to his room. Shortly thereafter the upper school padre, in the company of the head and the school nurse, knocked on Mr. Tracy's door. A few minutes later we heard, "And you can fuck off for a start, padre, and you too, headmaster, you jumped-up midget, and as for you, nurse…."

That apparently was when the padre and the head, who was very sensitive as far as height went, jumped onto Mr. Tracy. More masters arrived to subdue the enraged master, who managed to knock out both the head and the padre, and he was taken away. That was the last we saw of Mr. Tracy.

Many of us in the lower school would occasionally gaze in the direction of the upper school and wonder what horrors and happiness it held for us in the future. We would do one more year before our trek across the fields of play to the much larger world there. We already had seen our heroes play football, hockey and cricket, and we even knew a few of the names: Charlton, Newman, Jenner and Passi. They were giants in our minds.

Until then I had only met one real hero in my life, and that was Field-Marshall Viscount Montgomery. In the early 1950s he had come to Toronto to give a speech to the troops who served under him during the war in his new capacity as Deputy Supreme Allied Commander Europe, NATO. He was asked by the Queen's Own Rifles if he would visit their church and read the first lesson that Sunday, and since Father was the honourary colonel of the regiment, having won the DSO on D-Day that was presented by Monty, our family had the great man back to our house for lunch with a few select guests.

The entire family lined up at our front door to meet the hero of El Alamein. This small and taunt man in a field-marshall's uniform got out of the staff car in front of our house and ran up the steps towards us. Without a word outside of a quick handshake with my father, he seemed more interested in whether our shoes were clean or not, which thanks to Father, shone back at him. He nodded curtly to my sister and me as he proceeded to walk into the house, pour himself a glass of water and stand by the back window of the living room.

For a moment my parents were dumbstruck but snapped into action as the other guests began to arrive. My sister and I ran around taking the drink orders and making sure everyone had an ashtray nearby. In those days after church, it was all drinks and ciggies for both sexes and lots of both. The drinks were all hard liquor, such as scotch or rum, or the truly special

Canadian concoction, rye and ginger. No wine was served and I am not even sure Father had any in the house, although some of the more elderly women preferred sherry which Father always had around for his aging maiden aunts, Daisy and Jeanette.

Everyone smoked, mostly cigarettes, but some had pipes and one or two puffed on cigars. A few of the more refined women brought little engraved tins that served as personal ashtrays, but generally the children were kept busy emptying the brimming repositories. You could cut the atmosphere in the house that Sunday with a knife. Everyone wanted to speak to the visiting dignitary, so that Monty soon found himself surrounded by vast-bosomed women and hugely florid men. Our hero was a man of few words, such as "yes" and "no," which led to very short conversations, so that the bored crowd went back to talking amongst themselves, leaving Monty sitting alone on the far chesterfield. For a man like him who did not smoke or drink this party must have been hell, and he showed it by sitting ramrod straight and scowling. I couldn't resist the chance to be near him, so I sat down next to him. Our height was almost the same as he was no more than 5'3" or 5'4". We sat staring into each other's eyes almost on a plane for what seemed like minutes before he spoke.

"You have no doubt realized that I am not a large man?" he said.

"Yes, sir," I replied, but in a friendly way, with no cheek intended. He threw his head back and laughed, frightening my father into trying to pull me away as he thought I might have given the field marshall offense.

"Please, Colonel Clarke, young Robert and I were just having a quiet chat, no need for alarm. But could you push the window open a bit more as the smoke is becoming intolerable."

Father ran off, leaving us to ourselves. Monty looked kindly at me and continued, "Being small has its uses, young man. In fact it saved my life in the First World War. The date shall always be stuck in my mind, October 13, 1914, the First Battle of Ypres. Not so much a battle, more like a slaughter, with the dead piled up around me, a newly minted lieutenant in the Royal Warwickshire Regiment.

"I had, as ordered, blown my whistle at 7 a.m. and charged over the top of our trench, followed by my loyal lads, most of whom did not see the sun go down that night. I was hit after traversing some 50 yards and went into shock, lying in the mud amongst the dead and dying. As the sun came up, the German snipers got to work with deadly results, as we had no cover out on that field.

"My RSM saw my predicament and charged out of the trench that the troops still standing had retired to after retreat had sounded. The dear man was hit twice making his way towards me. He was a very strong and large as many regimental sergeant-majors are, and though he moved like a cat, it was no small miracle that he made it to my position, bleeding badly. With no thought for himself he threw his great body over mine to die whilst saving me. His body absorbed forty more rounds during the daylight hours, as I remained unharmed beneath him. Later that night I was saved by a medic and returned to England. So you see, young Robert, if I were not small, we would not be having this chat."

He had spoken quietly and matter-of-factly yet he had painted a horrible picture of war. Shortly thereafter he stood up, smoothed out his uniform, shook my hand and patted me on the head. He made his way to the front door, thanking my parents as he went, and was gone. He died at 89 in 1976. I enjoyed our chat.

All these memories from my childhood, filled with such promise. I know I disappointed my parents, who are both gone now, and what I could have become has been notably unfulfilled, yet I have tried in my own way to better myself. As someone said the other day, I have evolved into a character of some note, and I suppose I will have to be happy with that.

Like me, Canada has left most of its promise on the breakfast table and has evolved into a second-rate country, with leaders who are B and C players. During the Second World War, we had the most dreary of leaders in Mackenzie King, a former accountant for the Rockefellers who was terribly interested in the occult and talking to his dead mother and dog. In other words he was mad as well as dreary. When Canadians wanted to hear stirring words they would tune their radios to Churchill or Roosevelt. My father described waiting in the rain outside Buckingham Palace with 10,000 Canadian soldiers while Prime Minister King had tea with the Windsors and never gave a thought for his troops in their wet uniforms on what was supposed to be their day off. Two hours, yes, two hours of rain later, the PM came out on the balcony to deliver a speech to his loyal soldiers, and the men broke ranks and ran, booing, towards him. He quickly disappeared back into the palace as the MPs arrested many of the rebellious troops.

Many Canadians get teary-eyed at the thought of Trudeau and what he did; yet only two leaders of note appeared at his funeral, Jimmy Carter and Castro. Ah, this is thirsty work.

All the upper echelon of this country cares for are pensions one can double up on in Ottawa, and the same goes for the provincial capitals. When I was a boy, people would come from all over the world to study our educational and health systems. Now they come only to see how NOT to do it. When we trashed the Avro Arrow, our aerospace industry disappeared, and when we sold Connaught Laboratories where Banting and Best discovered insulin, that was the end of our research and medical genius. Our universities lose our best professors to the U.S. because we can't compete with their grant system, while our colleges worry about prayer rooms for odd religions and hang their heads in shame at the lack of lesbian poetry on their library shelves. Second-raters through and through.

I just noticed on the bulletin board that the lecture on global warming by Dr. Suzuki has been cancelled due to a snowstorm. If they want to save the world, close every golf course, as they continue to be one of the greatest wasters of water anywhere. Or shut down NASCAR: three hours of watching cars scream by, always turning left.

By God, I need a martini. There we go, it's on its way. Did I mention how I hate the English? Friends find my dislike of them amusing as I appear to be more English than most Canadians. It's my heritage. If my people had come from India and my house smelled of curry and I wore turbans, no one would bat an eye, except to say what a marvelous multicultural country we are. Bah, we have become a backwater. We have an English Queen and our Parliament is based on theirs, as well as our justice system. That's why people come here — not to wear funny hats, but to be safe.

The people who founded this place were crazed Scotsmen and indifferent Englishmen, and for a while we were a tough little country. Somewhere along the line we took a suicide oath and decided to have an undefended country and sell our jewels to the U.S.. who would defend us if something untoward happened.

Fear not, my drink has arrived and all is well. I do dislike the English, mainly for all the sacrifices we have made for them and their near total boredom toward us. Lord Black, a man who fell from grace made a wonderful debating point on a panel discussing newspapers in the U.K. on one of those BBC stations, either 2, 3 or 4, late one night. Some twit shouted:"What did a Canadian think he was doing, coming to the U.K. and buying a newspaper?" Lord Black eyed him for a while like a small bug, and then explained that there had been a tradition of Canadian press lords in England such as Lord Beaverbrook and Lord Thompson. Warming to his subject, he added that Canada needed no lessons from the British, having sent more than a million volunteers in two world wars to aid them. To their credit, the crowd gave the now disgraced Lord a standing ovation.

One Sunday afternoon when I was a boy, my father took me to the Sunnybrook Military Hospital to meet a man he often visited. He had been a bugler in the Boer War in 1900, and was originally from Estevan, Sask., having gone overseas at the age of 14. In his first battle he had taken a bullet to the spine that rendered him a quadriplegic. After that battle, the English colonel was heard to remark on the stupidity of the young bugler, where upon a Canadian corporal dragged him outside and gave him a good hiding. The corporal was almost shot for the incident, with Canada finally, with embarrassment, sending him home to jail instead. The country should have been outraged but no news got out. When the English wrote up the history of the Boer war, Canada was hardly mentioned.

My Father and I walked into the room of the tiny man who had laid on his back for more than 54 years, and few knew anything about him or that he was there at all. Canada turned its back on him. Yet here he was trying to salute my father as we came near his bed. He winked at me and with a twinkle said, "I'm sure the girls like you, my fine fellow." And laughed and laughed. He was the happiest person that I had ever seen with a personality as big as the sky. School children by the hundreds should have been lined up at his bed, not to be depressed but invigorated by this irrepressible optimist who by our standards had no reason to be so. But no, he was relegated to the back rooms of an old military hospital where only a few like my father came to see him. I am so glad I did and more than once. His name was Billy, and he died in 1967 of lung cancer, but I will always say he died by the shameful neglect of his country.

I have been finding that the club is going downhill a bit these days, have you noticed too? The staff looks shabbier and more morose, while the members themselves have taken on a taste for the lower orders. Shirts aren't buttoned up any more, ties are undone, shoes are thirsty for polish and there is a surly loudness to everything the younger members do. In short, a proletariat outlook is rotting the underpinnings of our once glorious club. We used to be so discriminating, and with style. I was telling my friend Reid of my worry and he was keen as mustard to do something when he suddenly fell asleep in his chair. Nothing takes the pepper out of one's argument than having the recipient cozying up to the Sandman while one is in full warble. But there it is, age. Reid is well into his eighties and is likely our eldest member, although I did spot one old crone behind the large vase near the main curtains who is becoming odiferous and needs inquiring about. She might be older than Reid, if she is in fact still alive.

Before Reid drifted off, he was complaining that a young member of the club was seen leaving the men's washroom having not washed his hands, which he claimed was not uncommon. Mrs. Crow, my dear nursery school teacher, insisted that all her charges sing Hickory Dickory Dock whilst washing our hands during our ablutions so that the length of the song determined the state of our cleanliness. Just before Reid's huge head sprawled onto his waistcoat I had begun a story, which I might as well finish. It concerns the cinema and my love of attending those dark amphitheatres. I so enjoy suspending my disbelief, as the term goes, just sitting back and being transported with delight. However I find the experience less and less to my liking, with the talking and the overall disregard for one's fellow cineastes. We used to be so excited when a Bergman or a Fellini movie was opening that we would go out in droves and silently read the translations at the bottom of the screen. If one spoke one was immediately shushed by one's seatmates as well as the usher's flashlight being shone in your face. Now the first thing that happens when one sits down is a pair of smelly size eleven sandals appear beside your head as someone settles in behind you. Followed shortly by his entire life story, which is banal, shouted over his deafening earphones, which he is still wearing. Just the other day I watched some filthy lad finish urinating, thankfully in the washrooms provided, and then, without even a glance towards the sink or the accompanying soap dispenser, he was out the door, smearing his hands on the exit as he went.

That was bad enough, but when I returned to my chosen seat well away from the rowdier elements I observed that same fearful boy putting his tattooed hand into the popcorn he was sharing with his female companion. I sank into my chair with revulsion and wondered if the women of this world ever ask their partners if they had washed their hands to "Hickory Dickory Dock, the mouse ran up the clock."

(This appears to be the end of Robert Clarke's diary. There was a rumour the other day that the old waiter at the club had secreted a further chapter or two on his person before resigning abruptly, but I have put that down to idle chat amongst the help. I would like to remind you that we have only presented this work and take no responsibility for its content. Ed)